"ACES!"

New York Daily News

"Offers cause to . . . rejoice . . . The Corringtons have a feel for place and history. . . . Memorable scenes linger in the mind."

The Washington Post Book World

"Racy, raunchy, gory, and written in language of the street . . . The Corringtons will have to do a lot to top *So Small a Carnival.*"

The New Orleans Times-Picayune

"What a grand old time the reader will have. . . . The Corringtons don't miss any opportunities to throw in liberal doses of local color. . . . Thoughts of the story linger days after the book has begun its rounds of friends who want to read it."

Sun Magazine

"A FAST-PACED YARN."

Salt Lake Tribune

SO SMALL
A CARNIVAL

John William Corrington
&
Joyce H. Corrington

FAWCETT CREST • NEW YORK

I assure you, doctor, it is a relatively simple matter for a weathered charlatan like myself to keep up interest in so small a carnival as this . . .
—NIETZSCHE

CHAPTER

1

*Man must have the strength to break up the past . . .
he must bring the past to the bar of judgment, interrogate it remorselessly, and finally condemn it.*

—NIETZSCHE

I PARKED ON THE BANQUETTE BEYOND THE LEVEE AND SAT
watching the sun drop toward the horizon across the
Mississippi. It was still hot and humid, and in the south-
west there were thunderheads pulsing and glowing. I
could feel rain in the air as I rolled up the windows and
climbed out of the car. A rain at dusk is a blessing.
Nobody who lives in New Orleans hates to see that
evening sun go down. Not in August.

Usually at that hour I'd have been working in the city
room at the *New Orleans Item*, or making the rounds of
the places where crime news happens. That's what police reporters mostly do.

But that evening, it was a little different. I had an
appointment at the Bethel Bar on St. Peter Street. Some
guy had phoned the paper, asked for Wes Colvin, and
said in a thin, distant, weepy voice that he had a story
for me, something incredible he wanted to tell me. He
had talked fast, as if he had to get it out before some-

body caught him on the phone—or before he talked himself out of talking. He had said something about a deduction box, and then rung off.

Nine times out of ten, I ignore anonymous calls. Even as I locked the car and started walking, I wasn't sure why I was paying attention to this one. No, that's not so. I was thinking maybe, just maybe, my caller had something about the Colombians.

That would be very nice. I'd been doing the police beat for the *New Orleans Item* almost five years. If I was going to move up and out, it had to come soon. I'd started back home with the *Shreveport Journal*, and then done a year on the *Baton Rouge Morning Advocate* before I came to New Orleans. The next step might be Houston or St. Louis—maybe even L.A. or Chicago if I came up with something flashy, something that got notices, picked up by the wire services.

The Colombians were my ticket. I was sure of it. These nut bags from south of the border had started coming into Florida in the high times of the seventies, and they'd turned the relatively easygoing Miami drug-dealing scene into Nightmare Alley overnight. There'd always been killings over big deals. What would you expect when two or three million bucks are in the sugar bowl? Little mama-papa operations moving two or three keys of cocaine or a big bag of horse were always getting wiped out by comers who had in mind to centralize the trade.

But not like the New Wave. When the Colombians hit a place, everybody died. Mama, papa, kids, old folks, any neighbor who raised a window wondering whose car had backfired like that. One guy from Miami vice had cashed in his pension and moved to the New Orleans Police Department just to get out of the line of fire. He told me they needed a search-and-destroy operation over there. When it gets that hot, he told me, you don't need cops. You need the military. You need stone killers. You need guys who can't get it up if they haven't wasted a dealer or two before midnight—every night.

For months I'd been hearing that the Colombians were coming over. Not that Miami had set their tails on fire. No way, Jose. Just that the Coast Guard and all the agencies had been screwing with their supply lines. They were going to add New Orleans to their territory, and start using the ten thousand bays and bayous and inlets from the Gulf to bring in their product without a lot of hassle from the feds.

I'd pulled every string and rung every bell trying to get some solid information. People I'd known for years, people I'd done favors for, were sick of hearing from me. Ralph Trapp in city homicide had found a new lick: whenever he saw me, he'd get this mock terrified expression on his face and moan,—The greasers are coming, the greasers are coming. . . . But so far, not a sign. Nothing special, nothing that would turn your head or your stomach.

And still I had this feeling. I wanted one clear shot at a series that would make the people at Columbia—the one you spell with a *u*, not an *o*—take a good look at me when they got together to mutter and mumble and back and fill and hand out the Pulitzers next year.

I stood on the long observation deck that overlooks the Mississippi opposite Jackson Square as the sun vanished and the sky went pink and gray and gold and scarlet. Maybe I should forget the career stuff, quiet my mind and settle myself once and for all in New Orleans. Buy a boat and go fishing when the weather was right, make the rounds of the bars and good restaurants every night, start writing that novel that every journalist in the country diddles with as a matter of ritual and tradition.

There was even a girl to fit into the early retirement plan. Sandy Greeley from Plain Dealing, Louisiana. She tended bar at the Bethel, and we'd been seeing each other whenever we could line up our off-hours. Sandy had glossy auburn hair, smooth silky legs, and a warm smile that stayed in my mind. She was good-looking and knew it, and had the notion that life could be a lot better than it had been so far. She worked nights at the bar and went to the University of New Orleans during the day. She kept telling me she might go to law school after she graduated.

It seemed a pretty good idea. Sandy had had some experience with the law. She'd married a scumbag from her hometown named Lester Grubbs when she was still a kid. It had been a very bad mistake. Aside from teetering on the edge of subhuman, Lester had the notion that all the movable property in Louisiana or wherever else he happened to be belonged to him by right. He spent as much time up on petty theft and burglary charges as most people do on the job. Once or twice, he'd even moved into aggravated assault with intent to maim. Then one day about five years before, without letting Sandy in on it, he'd elevated his own expectations. He'd left her outside in their broken-down '61 Thunderbird while he made a visit to the First National Bank of Commerce out on Jefferson Highway.

Lester had come out a lot faster than he went in, and he had two or three bank bags in his hands. Sandy had taken one look, and proved how smart she was. As he jumped in the passenger side of the car, she went out the driver's side and ran as fast as she could. Lester had taken Sandy's running off like that in bad part and had fired a couple of shots at her, screaming that she was a piss-poor wife and all he was doing was trying to help them get ahead.

Then, as he tooled off toward the River Road alone, one of the money bags exploded and sprayed red ink of some kind all over him, the car, and the environs.

Lester had been, as you might say, shaken by this turn of events and smashed the old T-bird into a telephone pole, mangling one of his legs and crushing his chest. When the parish sheriff's people came to collect him and the crimson currency, Lester was lying caught like a crab in a net between seat and steering wheel, muttering about the hard fate of a man who marries an ungrateful woman.

Lester had gone up to Angola, and Sandy had gotten one of the quickest divorces allowed under Louisiana law. A woman whose husband is convicted of a felony gets cut loose right then, as soon as she applies for it. In contemplation of the law, no woman should have to stay chained to a Lester Grubbs. It's the kind of statute that makes you feel a little better about some of the other lunacy the legislature dishes out.

Sandy and I had met a year or so after Lester's terminal goof, and from time to time we talked about some arrangement more encompassing than a night at her place, a night at mine. She wanted it and I wanted it, but that itch of mine, that drive toward Larger Things kept me skittish. When The Call from the Big Time came, I wanted to be able to throw everything I owned in a sports bag and catch the next cheap night-flight to my Destiny. I didn't know that Sandy would fit.

As I stood looking over the river thinking, I found myself getting into a humility mode. After all, genuine happiness doesn't mean nesting at *The New York Times* or the *Washington Post,* after all, does it? Yes.

Just then Jesus turned up.

—You looking down in the face, Jesus said.

—Just thinking.

—Never mind. You like a little hit? I got some vintage stuff. Champagne of cocaine.

—I'm a drunk, not a sniffer.

—Too bad. You pop a little of this, you know how He put the world together.

He called himself Hay-sous, but I liked Jesus. He played a little guitar here and there around the Quarter and looked like Leon Redbone. Probably on purpose. I had no idea where he picked up his ideas on dress, but you had to hand it to him. They were original. He always wore a white Palm Beach suit that had to cost three hundred bucks, a fine handmade Panama hat just a shade off-white, a pair of those dippy sun shades they kill for in New York—and a T-shirt.

He owned a T-shirt shop on Bourbon Street, and

aside from run-of-the-mill crap like MADE IN NEW ORLEANS, or IT'S RYE ON BOURBON STREET. Jesus could whomp up any zinger that crossed your filthy mind, and print it in italic script on a hundred-percent cotton shirt in ten minutes. He was wearing a diffident, tasteful number just then: ALL US CATS LOVE PUSSY. Jesus.

His people had made it out of Cuba just before Castro took over, and he couldn't even remember the place. But he wanted to remember, so he pretended he did. He could tell you how it used to be, about the harbor, the nightclubs in old Havana, the casinos, the bars and restaurants where the high rollers and deep-sea fishermen used to put in for drinks and a quick hustle with somebody's thirteen-year-old daughter. There was some kind of permanent built-in sadness in Jesus that seemed strange for a guy who'd just managed to get away in his mother's arms from hell in a small place. I used to tell him that, if his people had stayed, he'd be chopping cane right now, at night, under a searchlight while some guys with Kalashnikovs drank rum, whistled party songs, and watched him with their small beady red eyes.

—You going to Bethel? Jesus asked me as he sat down on a bench next to me and stared out over the darkening river.

—I'm supposed to meet some guy.

—Me too.

Jesus meant his brother. Ignacio belonged in some Latin James Bond film. He was just over forty and looked thirty, with sleek black curly hair and dark eyes that seemed to be looking past whomever he was talking to, brooding on some future, his or theirs, that was unspeakable, but which he would be able to bear because he had the capacity to bear anything, and it was expected of him that he should bear it.

Ignacio and I had an arrangement between us. I never asked him how he made his money, and he never told me. To me, he was the brother of a good friend; to him, I was a good friend of his brother's. We both knew I wasn't the kind of reporter who'd use a friendship to go digging and delving. There are four billion people out there with stories. Why pick on your own people?

But you hear things on the street, and the word on Ignacio was that he belonged to the old Cuban drug elite that had been handling fines herbes since they used to sell what they called reefers one at a time in the forties and fifties. It seems that marijuana had been handled by some of the same importers who brought in Cuban cigars before the revolution, so that the distribution network had remained in place when cigars were made contraband. If Ignacio's people could do their thing in the open, they'd have a big garish sign out front with some beautiful cigar-box label art on it, a monumental stalk of lush cannabis, and a motto, SINCE 1925.

Jesus and I never talked about junk. He always had a little something for friends, but he never sold it. You don't sell to friends. You do them services. Latins and rednecks understand these things. Ignacio told me once that when a society had gathered enough of what he called these "usages" together, you called it a civilization. It seemed to me he was right.

—It's been awhile, I said, almost wanting to ask where Ignacio had been keeping himself.

—Yeah. He moves a lot.

I risked stretching things a little.—He's not in trouble?

Jesus looked over at me, a little surprised. He realized my question was at the edge of *prudencia*.—You heard anything? he asked, with an edge on his voice.

—If I had, you'd already know.

Jesus smiled, and hit me on the shoulder.—Somebody with the DA's office talked to me awhile back. Sorry. I get nervous. Shit, I'm always nervous.

—Anything special?

—Yeah. I got no character, he said with a shrug. —Ignacio got the family *cojones*. I got a nice smile and a fast mouth. You call that fair?

I laughed.—We get what we need. If we stay where we belong.

—Ha. You sound like my old man. Don't take no

liberties. God put you where you belong. I tell him that's un-American.

—In America you mostly don't have to be nervous.

It was almost time for my meeting at the Bethel. We were up and walking then, as the clouds started to close above us, and thunder sounded and reverberated over the French Quarter.

We passed by the new Jackson Brewery building, watching tourists mill in and out, then crossed the street and moved on through Jackson Square past St. Louis Cathedral.

Bourbon Street was full of people and the sound of bands in the clubs on either side. Over the music I could hear more thunder in the distance.

—Rain coming, Jesus grumbled.—Keeps people off the streets. Fucks it up for the shops.

—That's a couple of hours away, I told him.

—Bullshit. Five minutes. Maybe ten. Nobody buys shirts when it's raining. They find some dump and settle in and drink.

—Come on, I said.—You want to be the first T-shirt millionaire?

—Yeah, Jesus answered, his eyes hard.—My first million buys a hit on that bastard in Havana.

St. Peter Street was quiet, the sidewalks almost blocked by parked cars. A block or two away, some bum in a dirty raincoat was walking fast as the glow of the streetlights suddenly came on. If you airbrushed out the cars, the neon, and a few other details, it could be 1745 or 1803 or whatever you wanted deep in the Quarter—if you wanted strange things like that. Down on the right, the Bethel Bar sign, carved out of hickory, had a gaslight on both sides. It wasn't a beacon like some of the things on Bourbon, but if you knew what you were looking for, that sign could guide you home.

As we walked, I felt the first drops of rain.

—You never told me who called you, Jesus said, walking faster.

—I don't know who, I told him.—Do you?

—Yeah. Sandy. She's got some news for you.

—It sounded like somebody sick, old.

—She's sick of getting old with nothing but the rain check you keeping giving her. She thinks maybe they not ever gonna get around to playing that game.

I shrugged. Sometimes I wondered if it wasn't better not to have friends close enough to read my mind.—You *did* talk to her, didn't you?

Jesus shook his head.—Naw, but I got you going, huh?

We both smiled. His was the real thing.—Yeah, I said,—But I'm going to do better.

His smile faded.—I don't think so, Wes. You Anglos all alike. You get something good for free, you don't give a shit about it. You got to work for it, kill for it, or it don't matter.

—You sound like a guy down at the paper, I said.—He can't write, but barroom philosophy is his thing.

Jesus shook his head.—All you poor bastards just the same. You don't believe in God.

—Sure I believe in God.

—No.

—What the fuck . . .

—Man believes in God, he believes in His grace. When He send you something good, you pray thanks and do right. No, you guys don't believe in anything but what you make with your own hands. Poor bastards. You think you gonna make something better than God sends.

When Jesus got into one of his religious snits, I tended to roll off. What could I tell him? Especially when he dragged my favorite barmaid into it. I believed just what everybody else believes. Whatever that is. God whelps those who whip themselves? Who knows? Who cares?

—Come on, I said, as the rain started falling harder. —I'm gonna off-load you on Ignacio, talk to my turkey, whoever he is, and then get to hustling Sandy.

—One of these days, Jesus was saying prophetically as we pushed open the door and walked in,—One of these days, she's not gonna be there for you anymore.

—That'll be the day, I started to say.

But as soon as we stepped inside, both of us knew something was wrong. The low backbar lights were on, the old-fashioned jukebox was playing a Glenn Miller tune, the name of which I had forgotten. There was no one behind the bar, and the mirrors back there were shattered. Bottles were sitting on the backbar, but the top halves of some of them were gone, and the rest were piles of glass.

—*Dios*, Jesus breathed.—*Mi Cristo* . . .

Later I'd remember that for a second, I didn't know what Jesus was moaning about. There were people at the tables, people in the booths, and in that dim light, I had to focus my eyes before my voice joined his in some kind of supplication, some prayer that it wasn't true.

—God almighty, I said.

Because at the table nearest us, I could see that the man sitting with his back toward the door didn't have a head. No head at all. Just a glistening, throbbing stump where you expect a head to be.

The table was covered with something that gleamed in the soft light, and the man sitting across the table was staring up at me with gaping glazed eyes as if I were some horror he'd been expecting, fearing, all his life. I remember his eyes because that's all I could make out. His nose, his mouth, his chin had vanished into a reddish-brown cavity that was still draining onto the lapels of his suit.

Jesus and I started moving from table to table then, trying to see what else was obscured in the shadows. It was worse. I could see as I looked across the room that people were scattered on the floor in front of the bar as if they had been told to lie down there. Some lay on their faces, one or two on their backs, open eyes catching the faint light as a cat's do in the dark. One man still sat or slumped at the bar looking like a drunk passed out. He wore a beautiful fawn-colored chamois coat. There was a line of six or eight small, dark, dripping holes stitched across the back.

There were people in three of the booths, all dead. In the first, a college-age boy and girl sat beside one another, eyes open, heads thrown back, still holding hands. They looked astonished, dismayed at what had befallen them, and the pattern of an automatic weapon that was sliced across both their bleeding chests looked like fine-linked chain binding them together forever.

In the second booth, an old man lay curled up against the wall looking as if he might have fallen asleep and missed whatever horror had passed through his neighborhood bar. But as I started to lift his head and turn him toward me, I could see the exit wounds in his back and shoulders, the padded seat behind pocked and splashed with blood.

I remember hearing Jesus somewhere behind me scuttling from table to table, sobbing and cursing in Spanish. Then he was over at the bar, and the curses were louder and harsher, with Spanish thrown in.

—Goddamn sonofabitch. Who does this? *Qué animal . . . ?*

Then I was at the third booth.

He was still sitting upright with great dignity. His left hand gripped the edge of the table, and his right hand was inside his custom-tailored jacket. The jacket had fallen open, one lapel plastered to the shoulder by his blood. I could see that his hand rested on the butt of an old Walther P–38. No, that's not right. His fingers, long and slender, curled around the pistol grip as if it were a musical instrument he was about to play. I remember thinking, He almost got it out of the holster. He almost did.

The bullets had torn a path through the table and into his belly and chest. I could see what he had wanted us to see. He had died well. His eyes were wide and fierce and sad and fixed on the door where we had come in. They were the eyes of a *torero,* one who had seen death and smelled it and managed to step past it many times before. Not this time. This time, it had come upon him too quickly, unexpected, beyond his power to stand aside or respond. This time there would be no more times.

I started to reach out and close his eyes. Then I pulled

my hand back as if his gaze had burned my fingers. It wasn't my place. There was someone else who should see his look, who should have his defiance to weigh against the loss.

—Jesus, I called out. Then louder,—Jesus . . .

But he didn't hear me, because as I called to him, he was calling me.

—Colvin, *ven acá . . . despacio . . .* Wesley, *amigo . . .*

I heard his call then, and he mine. I turned from the booth, and we looked at one another across the gloomy blighted room. He was standing behind the bar. We walked toward each other, and I think we embraced near a littered splintered table before he went to claim his brother and I to see to Sandy.

She was lying there on the wooden rails back of the bar amidst a field of shattered glass that caught the soft light from the backbar like winter ice, a little girl fallen asleep with her very best dream. She lay on her side, eyes closed, silent, modest, her skirt down over her legs. She had not been sexually assaulted, only murdered.

I curled the horror back inside myself and picked her up as gently as if someone might still be able to hurt or frighten her, jar her awake, back into a world where rooms full of people are butchered. I set her down on the plastic seat of an empty booth at an angle to the bar and tried to brush the broken glass out of her hair. I didn't see her wounds, and I didn't look. I thought if I saw where the slugs had pierced her, I might lose it, sit down on the floor sobbing and throwing up. I kissed her good-bye, and then I took off my jacket and covered her with it, trying speechlessly to explain that I had a duty to the living.

As I straightened up, I heard Jesus for the first time. I turned toward the sound of an animal run down by a truck, crushed beyond recovery. He was sitting in the booth cradling Ignacio's body in his arms, his white suit spotted with blood, his face twisted like a tragic mask.

It took a few minutes to get through to Rat Trapp at

police headquarters. Captains of homicide don't take their own calls.

—Yeah, he said in that smooth, hard black voice of his.

—Come on down to the Bethel Bar, you bastard, I managed to choke out.—The greasers are here. . . .

CHAPTER
2

I FOUND AN UNBROKEN BOTTLE OF GIN BEHIND THE BAR, and Jesus and I were doing our best to drink through it while homicide and the coroner's office did what they always do.

Captain Ralph "Rat" Trapp leaned against the bar like a bored customer, watching his forensic people work. The squad was young, high tech to their heels. On a crime scene, they could come up with stuff that God couldn't have found a few years ago.

Rat wore a dark three-piece suit, a lighter fedora, and one of those wide foulard ties I thought they'd stopped making. He was six and a half feet tall, with the build of a monster tight end. Rat had done ten years in the army, some of it in the military police, and the rest in a special unit in Germany that specialized in placing sharpshooters along the East-West border when word of an escape attempt from the East came down.

People who knew said Rat had himself a scoped rifle

rechambered to take the standard 7.62-mm slug the Vopos used. When people were coming across, and the East Germans shot at them, Rat would be in a tree or a dark window waiting. He shot back. Somebody said he had fourteen or fifteen Vopos to his credit—an American record. What I didn't know was whether Rat's unit was official, or just a pickup group of buddies who'd gotten permission to even out the odds. Nobody gave a damn. They just thought it was a very fine humanitarian idea.

Rat was a good cop. I should know. One time or another, I had come across almost every cop in New Orleans. Some were okay, a few were very good indeed. But Rat was in a class by himself. He liked to tell of the old days when he was growing up in the Desire project, when there were flower gardens and families, old folks and kids. When the housing projects were still a good place to be instead of the drug dens and slaughterhouses they'd become in the last twenty years.

The new situation didn't trouble Rat the way it did so many bleeding hearts. The ones who want out, get out, he told me. There's schools and little jobs, and there's the service. You reckon how many rich men started out to get theirs on the GI Bill? Free lunch went out with nickel beer. You give a man a chance, he takes it or not. If he does, send him on up. If he don't, fuck him.

I watched him watching the forensic people. You could tell by the way his eyes moved that nothing got past him. How could it? When other people went for their vacations like the last drink in the Gobi Desert, Rat made his yearly pilgrimage to the FBI Police Training School and learned the new technology—paying his own way. Some people thought they saw a future mayor in him. I doubted it. Rat could handle anything but boredom—and smart-assed reporters. He and I got along very well. We saw things the same way. He knew I wasn't looking for mistakes or police brutality raps. If Rat broke up a pusher, it was to get information he needed, not for giggles.

Once I'd seen him methodically work over a kidnap

suspect at a district station with the whole watch looking on. Rat asked questions and the scumbag laughed at him. Rat kicked him in the nuts so hard he lifted off the floor. Rat asked him again, and got a weak snotty answer. Rat hit him in the stomach hard enough to rupture his spleen. The next question got answered, and twenty minutes later, a little black girl was back with her mother.

The questioning had only taken five or six minutes. Nobody else on the force would have had the guts to put the questions just the way Rat did. But then nobody on the force knew he had the blood loyalty that Rat had. Did I report his methods? You want to sweat the civil rights of a guy who takes six-year-old girls and screws them for a while before he cuts their throats? Up yours. It's not that way no more.

Jesus was way ahead of me with the warm gin, and he was sprawled in a booth, his head down on his arms when the cops and forensic finished. Rat came over and sat down on the other side of the booth, almost pushing Jesus through the wall just to get room enough for his hips and shoulders.

—Aw, Colvin, you do beat all, he said to me with that tight warm grin that said all systems were engaged.

—Yeah, I said.—I wish to Christ I could beat the gunner who did this to death with his own piece.

—Well, you don't want to do that. Anyhow, it's gonna be awhile . . .

—I've been telling you for months the goddamned Colombians . . .

Rat shook his head.—I wish you could ease off that. You get to playing one note, and the *Item*'s gonna have to find theirselves a new boy.

—You're telling me . . .

—I'm not telling you a thing. We got it under investigation, like you see.

—I can save you time. They came in here for Ignacio, saw all those prime witnesses, somebody nodded, and they wasted the whole goddamned place.

I thought of Sandy then, what she must have felt in that last instant, and my voice closed down on me.

—I'm sorry about the little lady, Rat said.—I really am. They ought not do this shit with women.

—They ought not do it with anybody. If they want to blow each other away . . .

—Yeah. Maybe the Superdome on Monday nights or the racetrack off-season.

We sat quiet for a moment or two. Rat reached over and took a sip of my gin.—That stuff is terrible hot, he said.—You give up on ice?

—There was blood in the ice, I told him.—The guy with most of his head running over the bar . . .

—O yeah. You and your little buddy come here to see Ignacio?

—He did. I got a call . . .

Rat nodded.—So Jesus come to see his bruh . . . but you got a call.

—Some guy with a thin voice. Said he had a big story. Something about a deduction box.

—Deduction? What the hell does that mean?

—Sounds like something you check on a 1040, doesn't it?

—He never said nothing was going down?

—Not a word. Look, don't go playing detective and missing what those greaser bastards laid out in front of you. They'll do it again, just like in Miami. They don't care, Rat. They'll go in to pop somebody at Arnaud's Restaurant, and then waste everybody else in the place.

He gave me a cold look.—What do you say I get to play a little detective, old buddy? I mean, I got me a badge.

—Sorry.

—Nothing to it. You and your little friend got your own sorrows. Me? I got to check out everybody in this damned place and see for sure who was sitting on the rim when the tiddledywinks man come in. Rat sighed.—I guess I better go ahead and call the DA.

—Lemoyne? You going to shake him out for this?

—Yeah, I think I better.

—When he sees this place, he's gonna be pissed.

Rat turned toward the far wall where the ambulance

people had started to load bodies onto gurneys and wheel them outside.

—No, he said softly.—I expect he'll cry first.

—Huh?

—Yeah. You see the little old man in the second booth from the door?

—I saw him.

—That's Auguste Lemoyne, Drew's daddy.

The ambulance people were just lifting him from the booth then, laying him out and slipping a body bag over him. He seemed very small and older than the swamps, and you wondered what kind of animal had turned a machine gun on him.

—The old senator, Rat said with an elegiac tone to his voice.—Represented New Orleans in the state legislature before you were born. My granddaddy tended his lawn. Told me he would have voted for him . . . if they'd have let him vote.

I remembered the name the way I remember the names of Ivan the Terrible and Louis XIV, a label attached to some piece of time past that has nothing whatever to do with the life we're living now. Somebody who had done something in a time or place that made some other people remember.

—Outside of getting elected, what did he do?

Rat laughed.—Sometimes you white boys just put me away, he said.—Lemoyne, son, Lemoyne. That was Bienville's middle name, le Moyne. That old man's people was in Louisiana a hundred years before it was a state. Indians only beat' em here by a whisker.

—I didn't know you were into history.

—Oh, son, I do make it a rule to know the folks who've got hold of my chain.

Sure he did. Rat probably had a book on the mayor, the chief of police, the city administrator, and every other bureaucrat who could pick up the phone and be sure of getting through to him. That meant he knew about Andrew Lemoyne, the Orleans Parish district attorney. Know your employer-enemy. I feel the same way about Bob Pleasance, my editor at the *Item*. I wish

I had something on him. I'd be making six hundred a week and handling the entertainment beat.

—He was in the state legislature when Huey got elected governor. He was an Old Regular. Him and his friends and Huey and his friends was at each other for years, Rat said with an amused smile.—'Course Huey won out. He always won out till old Weiss closed down the game.

In Louisiana, there is a mythology of governance and corruption and violence that every kid knows before he is ten years old. Call it the Long saga. Take that any way you want to. A man from north Louisiana decided the poor people had been down too long. He decided the state belonged to the common man, that someone needed to tell the common man the truth of things, and then deliver over to him the keys of the kingdom of earth. But of course at the very moment of deliverance, when the long night of privation and hopelessness that had lasted from the end of the Confederate War until 1928 seemed over, one of the Uptown crowd killed him. They scattered his forces, imprisoned the good ones who wanted to go on with the plan, and put things back the way they used to be.

That's how the old folks remember Huey Long and his legacy to this day. That's how my people told it to me. Huey's name was another one of those names like Ivan or Louis—only closer, because my uncles and my father had seen his living face on the stump in Red River Parish and in Winn Parish. Huey Long was a myth, but he had been our myth, our martyred hero—even as he had been a demonic force of disorder to New Orleans and the Democratic Old Regulars.

They were wheeling the old man out then.—You wouldn't think he was history to look at him, would you?

—I don't guess, Rat said.—But then it only gets to *be* history when you're looking backward.

Rat rose to his feet slowly, easily.—Listen, I got a lot of work to do. Sorry again about your lady. When he wakes up, you tell your little friend we're going to find who did it to his brother.

Just then Jesus came around. His head snapped up, and he stared at Rat, tears still on his cheeks.

—No, because you ain't fast enough. I'll be roasting the fucker's nuts in a hub cap on an open fire when you get there.

Rat smiled, shrugged.—Haysus, you so bad. I got to remember to bring a bottle of Tabasco when I come to clean up.

He moved away then to check his troops. Jesus and I passed through the police and went outside. It was still raining softly, muted thunder whispering a long way off. A curtain of raindrops falling out of the night sky passed through the spinning light of a police car and made puddles of red on the wet street. We stood under the awning of a camera shop next to the bar and watched the line of parked ambulances blocking traffic in the street. The crews wheeled one body after another out, each one in its own black bag.

—I'm not bullshitting, man, Jesus said softly.—I know people. I can find out things. Something going down, I'm gonna find out.

—Maybe you ought to let Rat play it for a while.

—No.

—You afraid he might come up dry?

—I'm afraid he might beat me to the sonofabitch. I don't want no law, man. I want *justicia*.

I nodded. Jesus and Rat and I knew the difference. I reckoned that was why Rat hadn't warned Jesus off. If Jesus got lucky and found his man, Rat didn't give a damn if he tore him to pieces. If Jesus made a mistake, Rat would nail him, ship him to Angola, and never look back. That's how the big boys play out there in the streets.

—If you get something, let me know.

—Sure, he said, and walked out into the rain and down the street the way we had come. Sure, he'd let me know. Once it was over with and no one could stop him or even prove he'd had anything to do with it. You never tell your friends something it's better they don't know.

I waited for the rain to slack off, not because I minded getting wet. It was warm, and the walk might have done me good. But it felt as if I had to stay where I was till they brought out the last black bag. Some kind of a vigil. For Sandy, for old man Lemoyne, for that young boy and girl in the first booth. We need to invent rituals for sudden, violent, inexplicable death—since we don't have the balls to stop it. How can you say the same prayers for an old pensioner who dies at home heavy with years, and for two kids holding hands in a bar who never dreamed that their love was the best and last thing they'd ever have?

When the last ambulance pulled away, I didn't wait for Rat. The rain had almost stopped, and I started walking toward the parking lot where I'd left my car. The tourists and the locals on Bourbon Street were reaching their stride, drinking, yelling, laughing as they moved from one joint to the next with the jittering sound of phony Dixieland pacing them. It would go on till two or three in the morning. It always did. There was no season or time on Bourbon Street. It just kept going on.

Back at the paper, I paused in the hallway to pull things together. I could hear the presses down below winding up for the bulldog edition. The Bethel Bar wouldn't make that one. As I walked down the hall, I saw a light in the publishers office. Henry Holman would be in there, doing whatever it was he did late into the night every night. Holman was a latecomer to New Orleans. He'd only been here since 1930. But he'd done well, very well. It only went to show that a redneck from up-country could worm his way in, if he was willing to give enough of himself away.

This much I had to hand him: he was always there. Some of the boys on the city desk said the old man had a master computer terminal on his desk. He could read us as we worked if he wanted to. Then all he had to do was pick up the phone, say a word or two to Bob Pleasance, and a story got fixed, killed, or expanded—depending on how it might impact on him and the other members of the Pandora Club, New Orleans' social command post.

It sounded like liberal paranoia to me. For all I knew, Holman could be polishing off a fifth, waiting till he was sure his wife was asleep before he went home.

In the newsroom, the city editor, Bob Pleasance, had some kid monitoring the police band, and another one on the phone. Bob stared at me with that expression that said, You've just done your best buddy dirt. He wasn't my best buddy, and I couldn't afford to do him dirt. If I could, I would.

—This time you really blew it, Colvin. Maybe you ought to go back to Shreveport. Maybe this market is too stressful for you.

Bob's favorite line. He was city editor at the *Shreveport Journal* for years before my time. Then somebody down here died, they needed a quick replacement, and once on the *Item,* Bob held tight as a limpet. He even joined some carnival krewe and edged his way into the fringes of what passes for society in New Orleans. For some reason, he had it in for Shreveport—as if the town had played him false. I doubted it. He wasn't that much of an editor. Cold, cynical, always a step ahead of his reporters—and wrong half the time. But he paid his freight with the better sort of people by pruning out of our copy anything that might be embarrassing to them that wouldn't be a matter of general knowledge anyhow.

—I blew it, I said.—Again.

—There was a mass murder at a bar on St. Peter, he said, his eyes cold and mean.—I had to send Lucy Vaccaro from sports to Central Lockup for a briefing.

—Yeah, well, I said.—You win some, you lose some. Tell Lucy to check in with me when she gets back.

—What for? You want to tell her how the chop suey was at some fleabag in Jefferson Parish?

—Naw, I thought she might want some details, how it looked when it went down.

—What the hell are you talking about?

—The . . . what happened at the Bethel Bar.

—What do you know?

—I was there.

It looked like one of those commercials for some brokerage house. When Diddle and Droop talk, people listen. The kid on the phone hung up. The one nursing the police band turned around with his eyes crossed. Pleasance looked like I'd tied his dick into a Christmas bow. It was the only smile I managed to come up with the rest of the night.

After I dumped for Lucy, a cute little thing a year or so out of a local college Communications Department who should have been a groupie for Mick Jagger or Keith Richards instead of a reporter, Pleasance put me onto doing an obituary article for the old man, August Lemoyne. I told him maybe I should do the main news story and let Lucy do the research stuff. After all, fresh from college, with a degree in communications. But he knew what I knew about Lucy, so I started pulling up old papers on my computer, learning a lot that I never would have known except for my favorite bar being turned into an abattoir.

Rat Trapp had been right. The old man had cut quite a swath through Louisiana history back in the thirties. He and his crowd had despised Huey Long and dumped on him till all the rednecks and coonasses in the piney woods and bayous had come out of an eighty-year slumber and filled the ballot boxes to overflowing for him. After that, they'd feared and hated Long.

Maybe Auguste Lemoyne's biggest moment had been a speech in the legislature accusing Long of every kind of un-Americanism going the rounds back then. If Long wasn't a fascist, which he surely was, then he was an anarchist for certain, a communist beyond a doubt, and a socialist obviously—managing somehow to hold true allegiance to the tenets of every one of them at the same time. As I read the file, I laughed out loud. The speech was naive, silly stuff a sitcom wouldn't try today. But there was more to it than that. Under all the fustian and ranting, Auguste Lemoyne had been terrified of Huey Long. When I discounted the name-calling, there was still something there, and it smoldered fifty years later, as if the fear and hatred couldn't quite manage to flicker and die out.

As I finished reading the old file and cranked up my computer to write, I looked over through the glass panel at Pleasance's office. Henry Holman was in there. He and Pleasance were talking. Pleasance was nodding and nodding again. Something seemed to have upset Holman, and he was letting Pleasance know about it. I turned back to my screen and started writing. Their dipshit politics didn't interest me.

By the time I had an obituary, I found I also had an appetite to know more about the old man I'd found sitting in that booth at the Bethel Bar.

Pleasance listened, his expression revealing nothing.

—It's a good idea for a story, he said finally.—But it doesn't sound like your stuff. How about the Colombian zombie line?

—I'll stay with Captain Trapp on that.

—So will everybody else in town.

—I've got a few people out on the street, I told him. What I had was Jesus. But then he *was* a couple of people, depending on his mood.

—I don't want this two days after it plays on TV, Pleasance told me.

—Maybe newspapers are just for follow-up now, I said.—Maybe we just fill in the details after a story breaks on the six o'clock news.

Pleasance smiled. It wasn't a nice smile, but then I wasn't sure he had a nice smile.—Maybe you're right, he said.—And maybe we're overstaffed. If you *are* right, all I need is Lucy—and a couple of good typists. How many words a minute can you do, Wes?

My smile wasn't any nicer than his, and I can write longhand faster than I type. I left the obit with him, got hard copy of the old stuff on Auguste Lemoyne off the word processor, and found my raincoat in the left bottom drawer of my desk.

I went to Central Lockup to see what Rat had managed to scrape together. He was breaking up a detectives' meeting, so I asked him if the *Item* could buy him a steak. He laughed.

—You want to bribe me, now is the time. I feel like homemade shit.

We went over to Chris's Steak House on Broad Street. The steaks were good and the martinis were oversized and cold as the inner thighs of a Quarter whore. Rat drank on duty. Not a lot, but enough. He knew what happens to your guts if you let the tension build long enough.

—Okay, don't ask. I went by the DA's house.

—Better than a call.

—I guess. Who'd notice? They don't ask you to dinner when you come to tell 'em their father got wasted—along with twelve other people.

—What'd he say?

Rat stared at me as if I'd lost my mind.—He said it was a bad thing. He didn't like it.

—Gee . . .

—Naw, what he really said I wouldn't tell you except you'd find out somewhere, and I don't want to have to put up with you saying I told you so.

—Uh-huh. The greasers.

Rat sighed and finished his martini.—There's a lot of money going that way just now. Lemoyne says we got bad intelligence. He said the FBI couldn't find a shit-brown elephant in a snowstorm with its throat cut. Said we shouldn't even count on what we hear from the river parishes. Sheriffs either too dumb to breathe without help or on the take.

—Sounds right to me.

—You think the country boys would let 'em set up down there?

I shrugged.—What do I know? If you come at me with ten grand in one hand and a machine gun in the other . . .

Rat nodded.—I been wrong before.

—Not me, I said.—I've never been wrong. Not once.

We both laughed, and the steaks came, and we ate in silence for a while. Then Rat started talking on his own.

—Coroner's not done, and the forensic people still got a lot to do . . .

—But you've got something to chew on.

—Off the record. Not a word yet. Just filling you in for later, okay?

—You've got it.

—They pulled maybe fifty slugs so far.

—Umm . . .

—All nine-mm ammo.

—So you've got yourself a bunch of dopers with standardized equipment.

—More than that, Rat went on, the beginning of a sly look in his eyes.—Or maybe I should say less. They got slugs out of the old man, out of that poor bastard at the bar, out of an old lady down on the floor in the corner— and . . . Sandy.

Her name made me flinch. I'd managed to keep autopsy out of mind till then. If somebody invites you, challenges you to watch one, tell him to stick it. He's no friend. If they try to make you watch an autopsy performed on someone you love, blind yourself.—So, I said, keeping my voice level.

—Same gun, old buddy.

I didn't answer for a moment. I was trying to think it through.—You sure?

—Dead sure. You know what else? I bet every damn slug they put through ballistics looks just like every other one.

—What are the odds?

—What are you talking about? Ain't no odds. Reckon every morning it's a different sun rising?

He was right. Forensic had good people. If they said it was one gun, that was it—especially when they had a handful of slugs to compare. But the slugs had been drawn from people in every position in the bar.

—One guy?

Rat nodded.—Ummm. Looks like he reloaded after his first pass, and hosed down the place again.

Suddenly, I found myself with a headache worse than any I could remember. Maybe it was the warm gin.

Maybe too much happening too quickly. Or maybe the brain *is* like a computer, and headaches tell us there's an overload.

We finished, and Rat dropped me back at my car. I drove to my place uptown and took three or four aspirin before I tried some more gin. That must have been a mistake, because I had just one dream that seemed to go on all night.

Sandy was talking to me across the bar, her image multiplied by the mirrors behind. We were saying how nice it would be to go back home, back to north Louisiana, find a place on the lake, and fish together all the time. I could see other people behind me in the mirror, Jesus and his brother talking and laughing, a girl and boy just finding out they were in love, an old man smiling, remembering the long-gone days when people had listened to him, depended on him. All of us were happy somehow, and the drinks were flowing, and I was wondering why anyone would ever want to leave a place like the Bethel Bar.

Then something came through the door with a strange metallic clatter, and the room began turning red. I saw the horror in Sandy's eyes, and I came off the barstool and tried to get to the thing, whatever it was, but it was like swimming in syrup, and I knew I'd never make it, that the chuffing sound like a helicopter rotor was death itself, and when it was over, the laughter and the happiness would be gone, leaving me behind for no reason better than that, outside the dream, I had stopped to talk to Jesus instead of coming a little early for that appointment with whoever had wanted to talk to me.

CHAPTER
3

WHEN I WOKE UP, IT WAS BARELY FIRST LIGHT. I GOT off the bed slowly and fumbled through the routine of making coffee. I should have had a hangover ready for the emergency room, but it wasn't that way. Just a dull throb that I could live with—probably even work with.

I took the drip pot and a little candle-holder I use to keep it warm, and went out into the courtyard behind my place. In the early summer morning, before the sun is up and cars have filled the streets with fumes, you can smell whatever flowers are in bloom. The scent moves out across the neighborhood. Just then, there was some late honeysuckle, and the first blossoms of the second season for gardenias. Nobody ever invented perfumes like those, and I sat for a long time steeped in the odor of flowers, fresh coffee and chicory, mind blank, eyes closed.

Later, I expected I'd be tapping every loony and freak

I knew to find out the word on the street. There was always word, and I'd learned to respect it. You never managed to trace it back to first source—or if you did, you'd never know it. But even when it was off, it always had resonances. Threads led to patches, patches to a fabric. No one ever told anything firsthand, but everyone always talked.

After I'd spent the dawn without thinking, I went through old man Lemoyne's bio again. It made me think I'd have to check with Rat on the victims I didn't know. Not because I was trying to play detective on his mass-murder case. That seemed simple enough. The killers—or killer—had come for Ignacio. Maybe he'd even known them. At least he'd gotten a hand on his gun before they sent him away.

No, what I was interested in was which one of those thirteen people had called me just an hour or so before his voice was stopped forever. I could drop out the women—at least I thought I could—because it was a man's voice. I could drop Ignacio, because it hadn't been his voice, and he wouldn't have reached me that way. How about the guy sprawled on the bar? He'd looked like a gambler. Somebody who works pro ball games and the track might come across something interesting. What about the guy with no head, and his friend who had stared down the muzzle of his own dying and had even had time to realize it. They looked like lawyers or insurance people.

The hell with it. I couldn't even swear the voice hadn't come from an old lady they'd found lying in the corner. The only hope I saw was that Rat might come up with something on one of the victims that tied in to the phone call. Given that, maybe we could get somewhere.

In the meantime, I could pretend I was working by doing what I'd told Pleasance I was going to do: a nice nostalgic feature on Auguste Lemoyne, the New Orleans Democratic Old Regulars, and their losing war with the Kingfish. In fact, I was already doing it in my mind. Think what fifty years does to burning issues. Lemoyne and his buddies had been passionate about the threat that Huey Long represented to Louisiana—even to the whole country. People who ought to know say Roosevelt was afraid of him. It had been a knock-down-and-drag-out struggle in the legislature, the state house, the courts, even the U.S. Senate. Men had gone to prison. Long himself had died from an assassin's bullet in '35.

Now, half a century later, who the hell cared? The country had moved on. Louisiana was still here, more or less catching up with the rest of the country economically. An old man had died at an obscure French Quarter bar, in a cross fire between dope dealers whose interests he didn't even know about. In fifty more years, no one would remember the massacre at Bethel, or the reasons for it—even if the police nailed the perpetrator and sent him to the chair.

Henry Ford was right. History *is* bunk. We carry our own little piece of it with us, *our* history. What doesn't belong to us, hound us, devil us, doesn't make any difference at all. If I happened to be alive in fifty years, I'd remember Sandy Greeley. I might even remember old man Lemoyne and his story. The rest would be a blank.

It had gotten to be a decent hour by then, so I dressed and checked on the home address of the Lemoyne family. No use trying to reach the DA at his office. I'd tried that before in other situations. There were layers and layers of assistants and associates and paralegals and secretaries and press officers between the outer door of his office and the wood-paneled former conference room from which he directed New Orleans' war against crime.

A. J.-B. Lemoyne was a handsome, fifty-year-old lawyer with all kinds of money. Literally, all kinds. He had some old family money, whatever his father had managed to salvage from those days when Huey was taking them on his Louisiana Hayride. He had plenty from his own law practice representing insurance companies and corporate clients—and he lived now on the income from investments that shrewd lawyers get first crack at when they've made the right friends in the right places.

Drew Lemoyne was New Orleans' notion of an aristocrat. Like Rat Trapp had said, his people had been here since the creation. The Lemoynes didn't have to give much away to Jamestown survivors or Plymouth Rock types—much less New York Dutchmen. But they'd had some bad times between Bienville's time and the present. Drew's ancestors hadn't given a damn for the USA, and Louisiana's becoming a state hadn't thrilled them the way it had the English-Irish-Scots rabble to the north—my people.

The Confederate War had wiped the Lemoynes out, most likely. It had turned them from landowners to townsmen, and they'd been forced to make the transition from planters to lawyers and doctors. It must have been a bitter pill, but they'd done very well. The cycle had almost turned with Auguste Lemoyne. Only Huey Long and his crowd had stopped the old man and his confreres from buying back for a few bucks an acre during the Depression land that had been taken from them for pennies during Reconstruction.

Drew Lemoyne and his generation had closed the circle. The district attorney was rich and secure, handsome and popular. He hadn't announced for the governor's race next year yet, but he was going to. I knew he was, because that was the word on the street. The word was there hadn't been that much ambition closed in a single human skin since Huey himself. Lemoyne was already cutting deals with the black political organizations that herded votes for pay on Election Day. He was making speaking tours all over the state, and The War Against Crime was taking on fearful dimensions. Every time a cop pulled in a kid with a roach clip, there was a news release. Even Bob Pleasance, whose cynicism was depthless, found Lemoyne's publicity-seeking a pain in the ass.

It was almost ten when I flogged the brass knocker on the oak door of the Lemoyne home on State Street. There was no bell, just the knocker. Because no one inside really gave a damn whether they heard you or not. If it was important to them, they'd have heard it from their broker on the phone. If it was important to you, you'd be back.

A maid opened the door. Not just a black woman who mopped the place and washed dishes. A petite, good-looking woman in a black dress with a white lace cap. Maybe that's how it is among the high rollers in New Orleans, I thought. How would I know? I didn't spend a lot of time tasting the new Beaujolais or planning a ski trip to Vail with social types.

I told Fifi or whatever her name was that I wanted to see Mr. Lemoyne, that I was from the paper. She looked as if she didn't think my chances were great, but she let me in and led me to the library. Not the parlor or a den or something like that. The library. Three walls of books from floor to ceiling, and a fourth wall looking out into gardens that seemed more like a painting than reality.

There must have been an acre of grass and flower beds out there, tall green hedges, an ornate marble bench under a tall, perfectly proportioned magnolia. At one end of the gardens, under an immense live oak, between cliffs of hedge, I could see the end of a courtyard and a swimming pool. The rain had stopped for a while, and rills of water dripped from the eaves outside.

As I stood looking out, a girl seemed to materialize on the little corner of courtyard I could see. She wore nothing but a string bikini, and water was streaming from her long dark-blond hair. She was tall and slender with a body I wouldn't be likely to forget—long-waisted, small breasts, full thighs and calves, and a glowing suntan that possibly wasn't suntan at all, but the natural color of her skin. As I watched, I thought she might as well have skipped the white bathing suit. It concealed almost nothing. But as I watched her walking into the garden opposite the window where I was standing, I realized that the skimpy pieces of cloth made me want to see them fall away. The bikini wasn't wasted if she had in mind giving men dreams that drained them dry in the small hours of the morning.

The girl knelt by a blooming gardenia bush and drew some of the flowers to her. As she did so, a single beam of sunlight arched diagonally down, cut through the rain clouds, and shimmered around her like the glory in a medieval painting of the Annunciation. She felt herself bathed in the warm sun, and I saw her throw her head back and look up at the broken clouds. I had never seen a look of such anguish, such sorrow. What had seemed before a moment of pure joy was something else. She held the flowers close to her as if somehow she was telling them of her heartbreak, then she snapped off a single gardenia, cupped it in her hands, and began to cry. As I watched her from behind the distant window, I felt I had no right to be there. She didn't know I was watching her. I was a voyeur, caught in a dilemma. I shouldn't be looking, but there was no way I was going to turn away.

Then she stood up and walked to the weathered bench, the gardenia still in her hand. She paused there a moment, put the flower down on the carved marble, her head bowed as if she were praying. Finally, she turned to go back the way she had come, back past that sculptured live oak toward the sliver of courtyard far away, into a world I'd never seen. I found myself hard as the rock of ages, wishing I was one of New Orleans' better people. Just for an hour by the pool with her.

It began to rain again then, the library door opened, and Andrew Jean-Baptiste Lemoyne stepped into the room.

—You're Wes Colvin from the *Item*?

—That's right, Mr. Lemoyne.

He studied me for a moment, his eyes strong and focused, but something in his expression suggesting that his mind was a couple of miles away.

—I just called your editor, Bob Pleasance, at home.

—Oh?

—I told him I didn't appreciate one of his people dropping by my home when the family has just suffered a great loss. He said it was your idea, not his.

—That's right.

—Fine. Then I'm telling you what I told him. If you want to get along with the district attorney's office, you'll keep it in mind. Was there anything else?

I stared back at him, wondering if he knew how close he was to getting that patrician nose of his broken. He seemed to be laboring under the delusion that my job meant a great deal to me. Or maybe it wasn't a delusion. Maybe he was right. If he'd been wrong, why hadn't I already swung?

—I didn't come here to pick the bones, Mr. Lemoyne. I came within five minutes of being in the Bethel Bar when the butcher walked in.

He gave me a strange look. Don't ask what a strange look is. I know a strange look when I see one.

—You . . . were there?

—I have . . . I had a girlfriend. She tended bar.

—Dead?

—Everybody who was in there is dead, Mr. Lemoyne.

For some reason, he seemed interested then. No more uptown bullshit about dropping large hints on my editor.

—You were there . . . just after. Was anyone alive then? Did anyone say anything?

—The blood was still dripping when I came in. Nobody said anything. Somebody had called me.

—Called you?

—I was supposed to meet somebody at the bar.

—Who?

—I don't know.

His expression changed.—You . . . don't know?

—Whoever called didn't mention his name.

—Go on.

—Not much to go on about. I've been working on a story about the Colombian connection. I thought maybe the call had something to do with dope. He said to meet him at the Bethel Bar. He had something to tell me about the . . . deduction box.

Lemoyne turned away. I thought he was giving me a look at that silver-haired profile that would be popping up on election posters in about a year. No doubt about it, he looked like a governor. Maybe even a president—and maybe he felt the same way.

—Any idea what he was talking about?

—No. All I know is one of those people in the bar wanted to see me, talk to me. If I'd been there earlier, I'd have found out what and who. And I'd be dead.

He seemed to mull that over for a moment. Then he looked up at me as if I was ripe for cross-examination.

—Funny that you're so sure.

—What?

—What makes you certain the person who called you was in the place?

I know I turned red. Because that thought had never crossed my mind. I hadn't considered the possibility that my caller had never made it.

Lemoyne saw that he had me going. His smile was wintery, distant. He could calculate every turn and shift, every falling-off and misadventure of the human mind. He had been there, prosecuting the turns and shifts.

—It didn't occur to you that the shooters missed their target? That they killed thirteen wrong people?

They say I play good cards, but I'm a talent man, a luck man. Nobody ever put me up for the poker-face award. I just stared across at him, something ugly and lost churning my guts. What if my caller hadn't made it? Maybe never even intended to make it. Maybe . . . had called to set me up. I thought it through, then pushed it out of the way.

—No.

—You're sure of that?

—Look, I said, my voice louder, shriller than I intended,—I don't know anything. I don't have enough to fill one balloon in Believe It or Not.

Lemoyne knew he had me. He shrugged, looked out

into the garden where the rain was falling steadily now. I'd never seen him operate in court. I thought he must be awesome.

—They say the Colombians kill whole families . . . on suspicion. You know Charlie Sayers in narcotics?

Yes, I knew Charlie Sayers. He was the guy who had come over from Miami. For shelter. I didn't answer— which was answer enough.

—Well, Lemoyne said, after letting me steep in it for a moment,—like they say, I'd rather be a player than an innocent bystander. Was there something specific you wanted, Mr. Colvin?

It took me a second or so to find my voice.—We were thinking of a feature on your father.

—A feature?

—He had . . . an interesting life.

Lemoyne walked to the window. The cool rain and the warm earth were generating a soft mist that eddied among the gardenia bushes. We both stood looking out.

I tried to evoke that golden girl I had seen twenty minutes before, but Lemoyne had something else in mind. He pointed to the weathered marble bench near an arbor covered with white wisteria. The one the girl had placed the flower on.

—He bought that bench in Florence long before I was born. I remember how we lugged it from one rented house to another when I was a boy. He said one day we'd have a fine garden like his grandfather had had. He said he'd sit on the bench and take the air on a spring morning.

Lemoyne turned to me, his face cool, expressionless.

—I think we'll pass on the feature article, Mr. Colvin. I have a public job, but we're a private family. My father lived his life . . . and died his death. Maybe there'll be another time for your piece.

I nodded. He'd done a workmanlike job on me, and just then all I wanted was to be out of there, to get loose so I could think instead of feeling.

—You'll excuse me now, Lemoyne said, lining me up

for his last shot.—I have to go make arrangements to bury an . . . innocent bystander.

I drove downtown by rote. If you asked the route I took, I couldn't tell you. There might have been six or seven fatal crashes along the way, a trolley or two derailed, the Pontchartrain Hotel on fire. I kept trying to get past the possibility that Sandy, old man Lemoyne, Ignacio, and the anonymous others had died because some lunatic with a submachine gun, who didn't know me, thought I was sitting at a table in the Bethel Bar.

My feelings said maybe, but my brain couldn't buy it. I'd told Lemoyne I didn't know anything, and it was true. I had a collection of clips from Miami and south Florida, a handful of unrelated junk I'd picked up from Rat Trapp and Charlie Sayers. I had bits and pieces of street talk that might add up when I got some more, when somebody dropped in just the right bit.

Which is to say I had nothing. No journalist working on a neighborhood giveaway paper could write a piece from what I had that would say more than that a lot of dope was coming into the country, much of it from South America, and some of the top pushers were kill-crazy junkies reputed to be from Colombia. Nobody goes around wiping out a baker's dozen of people for that.

But wait. *I* knew what I knew. But whoever paid and aimed the machine gun didn't. Was there the thinnest of chances that some greaser with stewed prunes for brains thought I knew more? Or didn't give a damn what I knew, but meant to make sure I found out nothing?

It was still thin. Hitting reporters is like hitting cops. All of a sudden, everybody's interested and looking. Easy gets hard. What nobody paid much attention to is instant front page. Never mind taking care of our own. A dead reporter on a story can sell a lot of papers. But maybe the crazies didn't know that. Maybe they believed you could scare off the papers and TV if the casualties started mounting. In Colombia, in Sicily, in the Arab countries that makes sense. Who dies for a by-line? Americans do.

I couldn't believe it, and I couldn't get rid of it. All I could do was keep probing, digging and delving. And watching my back, paying careful attention to strangers.

Jesus was waiting at the Café du Monde. He was spiking the black natural coffee with rum, but he was cold sober. His eyes were dark and hollow.

—Nothing, he told me.—Not a whisper. Nobody hinting nothing, nobody spending. Just another day in the Crescent City.

—No price change?

—Nope. Come on, you know I know what to look for. Everybody sorry, nobody know a goddamned thing.

—Keep pounding, I told him.—You can't pull off something like last night and keep it a secret on the street. Did you ask if . . .

—Anybody doing a deal for automatic weapons? Come on, man. I even got names of people who drink at Bethel. Nothing there. You gonna see Trapp?

—Yeah, if I can. This is going to be a bad day for him.

Jesus gave me a cynical smile.—I got this big throbbing pain in my ass for him. He's gonna have a bad day. I'm going to bury my brother.

After I left Jesus, I checked in with Pleasance. Just to make sure he didn't empty my desk drawers and put somebody else on the beat while I was fumbling around. He wanted me to see Rat, too.

I was going to give that a try, but first I had to go by the Dickson-Turner mortuary and make arrangements to have Sandy shipped back home to Plain Dealing when the coroner released her body. I didn't think she'd want to be buried in New Orleans. But then I didn't know what she'd want. We hadn't quite gotten to the point where you exchange funeral plans.

When that was done, I tried to edge my way into Rat's office. One of his uniformed people pulled me aside.

—He's working out of his car, Wes. Look . . .

The hallway was jammed with people. I recognized the Atlanta stringer for *Time*, some guy with a nasal accent and hair that had to be set in place with shoe polish who worked for *Newsweek*. Cable news people, network people. Rat was right. If he turned up here, he wasn't going to get any work done.

—You know where Sally Marshall's place is?

—Sure, I told the cop.—It's the place we don't tell tourists about.

He laughed.—Captain's gonna check in there for lunch. Said if I saw you, pass it on.

I thanked him and headed for midtown, for a black neighborhood that used to be high rent and silk stocking. The houses were enormous and had once been beautiful and ornate. Now they tended to look like derelicts, hulks parked forever in a ship's graveyard.

Some of them were three stories tall, with bric-a-brac and balconies and gingerbread carving, bow windows. They looked like abandoned steamboats left huddled by a shift in the river's bed, each one carved into eight and ten little apartments now, unpainted, woodwork decaying. In one of them, Sally Marshall had opened herself a Creole restaurant. Not a po' boy sandwich joint or a beer bar. Haute cuisine of a very particular character. You didn't bring people from New York or Houston to Sally's, and they sure as hell never found it on their own.

Rat was sipping a beer and examining the menu with a frown. I stopped a little way from his table and looked him over. If you didn't know he was a cop, you could be talked into believing that he ran black crime hereabouts. He was dressed in a tan double-breasted suit with a dark brown silk shirt beneath it, and a tie that looked like it had been spun from old gold. The shoes were bison or elephant or some other exotic critter, and over the back of the chair next to him was an umbrella with fabric that matched his suit. He looked up, saw me, and smiled.

—You waiting for an invitation?

—Naw. Just wondering how you can afford those clothes.

—I'm a careful man with money.

—Nobody ever asks you whose money?

—Shit, Wes. You decided to get off the greasers and onto the brothers?

We both laughed. Rat was clean. He did know how to handle money. For years, even when he was in the army, he'd poured most of his pay into his cousin's construction company. Now it was paying off. It was cousin's turn to start sending some of the bread back across the waters.

Rat looked back at the menu.—I think the pigs' feet.

—Sucker.

—Oh?

—Neck bones and gravy. Stay with a sure thing.

—Hog's lips, yams, and dirty rice. Side of boiled river shrimp to start.

—Just stay away from the chitterlin's, or I'm gonna find another table.

—Chicken necks and potato patties?

—The neck bones are where it's at, neighbor, but if you're experimenting, do the lips. Ask for a side of sour cabbage or the mixed greens.

We negotiated a meal, got a pitcher of Dixie beer, and settled down for the New Orleans version of a three-martini lunch. It's a big world. There could be better food. Tell me about it. I'll buy my own ticket. We ate without talking, and when the last hog lip and neck bone vanished, along with the cabbage and dirty rice and corn bread, we sat there staring at each other, satisfied. Or maybe the word is surfeited.

—Your forensic folks all done?

—I may fire the whole goddamned bunch of 'em.

—Why? They're good people.

—They ain't worth a shit on this one.

—Nothing?

—All they give me was what I already suspicioned. It was a one-gun job. Somebody with a MAC-10 marched in and opened up. No questions, no loud voices, no argument.

Rat squinted at me.—Did youall stand around outside the bar talking before you went in?

—I don't remember. We might have.

—Then you could have been out front while he was shooting.

—Huh?

—Striations on the slugs say a silencer. Loudest thing you would have heard was the bottles and mirrors breaking up.

—Register?

—Maybe two hundred bucks still in it. Gabe D'Anolfo owns the place. Got him a little safe in back. Not touched. Cat blew everybody to hell before they knew they was going, then went out the back, over a fence, and bye-bye. Bastard could have been wearing a tux and carrying his piece in a violin case for all I know.

—Staying up late for the old movies, huh?

Rat was thinking. He looked suddenly tired, down.

—This could be the one that kind of throws me off track, buddy.

—What?

—I've been going up for years. Didn't know what down was. Once they took the seg monkey off my back and let me run, I never looked back. But I got a bad lowdown feeling this is the case that's gonna settle me right where I am.

He wasn't kidding. Since all the civil rights hoopla had freed up open spots on the force, Ralph Trapp had been jumping a grade every two years or so. Part of it was politics, but the big part wasn't. He was good, he knew what he was doing, and if he said the Bethel shootings gave him a chill, I believed him.

—There's got to be something. You told me a long time ago, there's *always* something. Nobody can pull off a mass murder and then go back to breaking in grocery stores and stealing canned goods.

He shrugged.—I know what I told you, and you ought to know I was bullshitting. There's always that one that breaks the rules. I wish to hell you'd called Teddy Davis.

Davis was another captain in homicide. White, dumb,

snot-nosed, and brutal. The only thing I'd call him was a miserable sonofabitch. But if I'd thought the case was going to go sour right up front, I'd have asked for him when I called from the bar.

—What about the people? I asked him.

—That's when I started getting this bad feeling. You got two salesmen from Kansas City . . .

—One with no head, sitting at the table nearest the door.

—Uh-huh. And the old lady on the floor kept books for D'Anolfo and took out her pay in booze. Couple of Tulane kids, one from Tulsa, and the other from Wave-land.

He stopped, looked down into his beer.—Wes, except for Ignacio, it's a blank. We're going to keep asking, but what you see is what you get. And it looks like Ignacio's out of it, too.

—Why? I thought . . .

—I know what you thought. The truth is, either Ignacio was bullshitting Haysus, or Haysus been bull-shitting you. Ignacio dealt his last junk over a year ago. He's been making deals on containerized freight down at the port of New Orleans. Unless he made a real bad enemy awhile ago . . .

I was surprised. But I began to realize what Rat meant about a bad case. Ninety percent of the nondomestic cases homicide closed with a conviction solved out by motive, by street talk, because someone spent or some-one bragged. No motive, no solution. Unless some poor bastard of a killer made a really stupid mistake—like pissing off his girlfriend. I dropped some money on the table for my side of the tab.

—Maybe you'll hear something, I said.

—Maybe I won't. My people have been twisting arms and beating on ears since ten o'clock last night. Not a squeak, baby. Nobody knows . . . and the worst part is, I believe 'em. There's nothing out there.

Rat fell silent again, and I finished off my beer.

—It's out there, I said, but he wasn't paying any

attention. I waved to Sally, kissed my fingers to her over the neck bones, and walked back outside.

The sun was out. It must have been ninety, and it felt as if I was swimming instead of walking. That's August in New Orleans. But my mind was on other things. It's out there, I said to myself. It has to be, because nothing goes down without a trace. That sounded fine to me. I just wasn't certain it was true.

CHAPTER
4

BACK AT THE OFFICE, THERE WERE PEOPLE HANGING off the walls. All the network types who'd been looking for Rat at Central Lockup were looking for me. I'd never thought of that possibility. I was just eyes and ears and two fingers to punch the keyboard, but one of the kids who'd been working the story met me at the elevator when I got off at the newsroom, and pulled me into the executive office hallway.

—Bob says he wants you to lose the city room. Maybe you ought to take one of the portables and feed us whatever you've got from your place by modem. All you're gonna get in there is twenty-two dips from the nets and the big papers wanting twenty-nine hours of your time for free.

I smiled.—You mean twenty-nine hours of my time that belongs to Pleasance.

—You got it. Need anything from records?

They used to call it the morgue, but now it's computerized, and you can call up whole reams of the paper's back files running behind the Confederate War with a couple of typed lines and a tap on the execute key.

—Nope. Where's a portable?

The kid produced a small suitcase, a box of floppies, and I was on my way. All the hotshots from the big time never knew the Witness had come and gone.

At home, the sun was filling my courtyard, and bees were hitting the four-o'clocks and late honeysuckle. I set up my machine, shook out the hard copy I had on Auguste Lemoyne, and almost tapped out a first line.

Then I realized two things were missing. A gin and tonic in a quart mason jar I keep at hand so I won't have to refill every ten minutes. And a little more thought on what and who I was writing about. An old teacher of mine at LSU, the best professor of American history who ever was, had written a biography of Huey Long. It probably had some stuff on Lemoyne in it. I wished I'd bought a copy now.

Never mind. If I found I needed it, I'd pick it up at the library and skim it. I never read anymore. I skim. What something means doesn't matter. Only what it looks like it means.

Auguste Lemoyne, born 1900 at Touro Infirmary. Jesuit High, Tulane, and Tulane Law. Attorney, elected to the legislature in 1928, the year Huey was elected governor. Lemoyne had gone in representing the Old Regular New Orleans interests that liked things just the way they were. The next year, they'd tried to impeach Huey. They failed, and in return he broke them, their machines, and even their business interests. Some of them, who couldn't learn to shut up and let him govern for the people, got themselves chased out of the state.

Reading through the old files, it was surprising how many names I recognized. New Orleans names, Shreveport names, names of families I'd heard of in Baton Rouge while I was in school and later, working for the *Advocate*. I leaned back, sipping my gin and tonic, thinking none of us is an end in himself. Just another link in a human chain that comes from God knows where, going to nobody knows. There are young lawyers working in New Orleans today with the same names as those I was reading about in newspapers dated April 29, 1928, August 7, 1929. Then a by-line caught my eye. Henry Holman. He'd been a reporter in those years. He'd come a long way. Most reporters don't end up owning the paper. I envied Holman. Not because he owned the *Item*. I was thinking how it must have been to cover the Long years, wishing I'd had a chance to talk to old Auguste Lemoyne—but not at the Bethel Bar.

The heat had dried the courtyard outside, and it was welling in through the door. I pulled the long cord I had connected to the ceiling fan and took off my shirt. I don't like air-conditioning, but one of these days, if I stay, I thought, I'm going to have to give way.

Once I finished the feature, the next step—if there was a next step—was to get the names and addresses of the other victims from Rat, and check them out, one by one. I'd leave Ignacio to Jesus. If there was a pinhead of proof directed at anyone, he'd come up with it. I was hoping—but not betting—he'd check it out with me before he went into overdrive, flew back to Miami or wherever, and arranged a hit. He knew as well as I did there was a big justice to be done, and not only for Ignacio.

The heat and the booze had carried me down to the edge of sleep, and I slumped over the computer keyboard. In that border zone between sleeping and waking, I was already walking through a static unreal landscape designed and built by aliens to resemble St. Peter Street. Out ahead, I could see the Bethel Bar. I tried to check my watch but I didn't have any arms. I didn't have anything at all. I was disembodied, on my way to where my dreams kept taking me, powerless to turn aside or even hope that I might be there early this time, armed to the teeth.

The door buzzer brought me back up from that depth,

and its sharp insistence that I had always hated, promising myself to change it for a diffident chime, seemed just then like a blessing. I got up and tried to reach the door before it sizzled and snarled again. I didn't quite make it. Perhaps a habit picked up in my dreams. Then again, I thought, when I opened the door, I'm not out of my dreams. The bad one had somehow got derailed. This is the good one, but it's not real, either.

She was standing outside the screen door, her hand just retreating from the buzzer, both arms filled with what looked like enormous artist's portfolios. Her hair was the same strange gunmetal blond color accented with a gardenia, but now I could see that her eyes were green, her lips a soft pink against the dark peach tint of her skin. She wore a one-piece white cotton dress that looked like one of those dusters people wore riding in autos at the turn of the century. It obscured the lines of her body, but that didn't matter. I'd seen all the rest before.

—Mr. Colvin, I'm Denise Lemoyne.

—Yeah, I almost knew that.

—Sorry?

—I think I saw you this morning. In the garden at your place. When you were picking a gardenia.

I think she blushed. Maybe I should have. But what the hell? In dreams, you can say anything you want to. It means something else anyhow. Doesn't it?

—Oh, she said at last.—I don't wear that suit when I have guests.

—Too bad. But I wasn't a guest. Your father made sure I got that much clear.

—I know. That's why I came.

I opened the door for her and took the big folios, which turned out to be crumbling old scrapbooks loaded to overflowing with clippings, pictures, circulars, documents.

—What can I get you? I asked. If I could keep this dream going long enough, it was going to be the alltime triumph of my sleeping hours. Maybe I'd figure a way never to awaken again.

—Whatever you're drinking will be fine.

—Gin and tonic with a splash of Rose's Lime Juice. In a mason jar. You can have a glass.

When she laughed, her nose crinkled, and her eyes almost closed as if she expected to be kissed. I wondered how it would feel to be dancing with her at some country club, alone on a terrace, kissing her as she laughed. I tried to make it happen with my mind, but nothing changed. I began to believe I was awake.

—I think the jar will be just fine.

—Just the way you drink at home.

—No. I think Carole uses Ball jars.

We both laughed. She had the slightest touch of a New Orleans accent. I didn't have to ask whether she had conversational French. Anyhow, if I'd asked, she'd have responded in French, and what would I do then?

I handed her a jar and watched her eyes move around my place.

—First bachelor pad you've ever seen?

—Ummm . . . I always try to find people in their rooms, the places they stay.

—Good hunting, I said. No one was going to find me there. Because I wasn't. I had a big apartment in New York or Washington, London or Paris. A couple of bedrooms full of good Louis XV copies, a living room that defined eclectic—Old English corner chairs and a hunt board cheek by jowl with Plexiglas tables, floor-to-ceiling windows looking out on an incredible vista, a study with a ragged but impressive working library, a few drawings worth small bundles, and maybe one Paul Delvaux that I would be paying on for the next thirty-three years. None of that was here. It was all stored in my imagination.

—Nope. Denise Lemoyne shook her head.—Never here—or gone. No forwarding address.

—I'll be sure you get it—as soon as I've decided where it'll be.

—You're not going to stay in New Orleans?

—Not even if I die. I've left instructions.

—You don't sound like a Yankee or . . .

—North Louisiana. Shreveport.

—Oh.

I could tell she meant, Oh. One of those. New Orleanians share with New Yorkers the peculiar delusion that their patch of ground is the heart's desire of everyone else in the world. But they know there are rare unregenerate exceptions. As to New Orleans, north Louisianians fall into that class. But Denise seemed cheerful about it all the same.

—Well, if you're going to be around another day or two . . .

—It might stretch out to years, I told her.—I could make a commitment—hard and fast . . .

—I'll bet you could, she smiled. But then she reached for one of the big scrapbooks.

—I came to say my father's changed his mind.

—Sorry?

—He said you wanted to write an article about my grandfather.

—That's right.

— . . . and he told you no. We talked about it, and he said all right.

—You mean you talked him into it.

She shrugged and opened the book.—These are his things. He kept letters, political circulars, photos . . . almost everything.

—He had quite a life, didn't he?

Denise nodded, silent. I'd wondered how much losing her grandfather had meant to her. Now I could see. She took a belt of her drink.

—He deserves . . . something. Maybe an article is all there is.

—I write good articles. It's not the *Cambridge History*, but it beats a lite beer commercial.

—I know. I saw your stories on the craftsmen of New Orleans.

I'd done a three-part series on old folks who still plied the dying trades: plasterer, cabinetmaker, wrought-iron worker, fine carpenter, stone carver. Maybe I was prouder of it than I should have been, but I wondered if I'd ever do anything better, deeper, finer.

—The end made me cry, Denise said.—I remembered it again when Daddy told me about . . .

She paused, and then spoke softly, just above whispering.—They never worked for money alone. One look at the work itself tells you that. They worked the way men worked in the Middle Ages. Because work was a great good, and worthy of a man and a man's dignity. They made mute stone and wood and plaster into beauty—a carved stairway, a lacy balcony wrapped round a second-story gallery with a delicate intricacy no one has a right to expect from metal, a gold and ivory and amber ceiling that wasn't gold or amber or ivory at all—simply plaster and paint and artistry. But the stone is harder now, the wood less yielding, the plaster unwilling to obey. They are old, and it is late, and there is no one to follow. . . .

There were tears in her eyes. She remembered what I had written better than I did. I wondered if those were my words or hers. I hoped they were mine.

—Christ, I said, without thinking.—Somebody reads it.

—I think of him that way. He loved the city, and he fought so hard for it.

—You know what he did? He was out of politics before you were born.

—I wrote a senior thesis at Newcomb College before I went to law school at Tulane. In southern history. It was called "The Long War."

—New Orleans against Huey.

It was her turn to look surprised.—What do you know about it?

—I come from what you folks would call an oral culture. They still love him out in the country, in the northern parishes.

—It's all a legend now.

—Okay, if you can put up with my fables, I reckon I can stand yours.

—You . . . admire Huey Long?

—I admire what my father and my uncles used to tell me. Every time I see my utilities bill, I admire anybody who went after New Orleans Public Service, Incorporated.

Denise almost dropped her mason jar as she laughed out loud.—God, I can see why my father didn't warm up to you.

—Don't blame him. I should have waited a day. He's out a father, and he's got thirteen killings to prosecute.

She looked somber again. It was hard to decide when she was more beautiful—happy, sad, serious, laughing. Like the rest of us, Denise Lemoyne had moods. Her beauty wasn't subject to them. I wondered if that certain quality about her that made my breath catch in my throat was something you picked up from life if your people were rich, and you could spend all the hours you wanted sunbathing in a white string bikini by a pool ordinary people never saw.

—Daddy said you were there . . . at the bar when . . .

—Not exactly. I'm still alive. I was there . . . just after.

I knew what she wanted to ask me. Maybe it was the real reason she had come. Something her father couldn't tell her. Something she wasn't going to ask and had to know.

—You loved your grandfather, didn't you?

She nodded.—More than anybody. When my mother died, he took care of me. He made me be happy, no matter what. He taught me how I could always be happy if I wanted to.

—More than your father?

Her eyes veiled themselves. My sensors caught the least bit of reticence.

—I love my father very much. It's just that . . .

—Never mind.

She was still waiting.—It was like he'd gone to sleep, I told her.—You know how elderly people will drift off sometimes? Like that.

She nodded, and I could tell she was relieved. I remember thinking how often I had seen dying—or just after. It almost never came quietly or gently. Or even bearably. It came titanically, hugely, terribly. It was almost always as awful as we expect it to be. When we have the guts to think of it at all. If you could judge by the faces of those just dead, it came as an astonishment, as the last and final disappointment. Of all the dead I had ever seen—in war, in hospitals, in endless shootings and carvings on the streets of New Orleans—the old man was the first who looked as if he'd fallen asleep. Had it been otherwise, I'd have lied to Denise like a gentleman. It was nice to tell a soothing truth.

—That makes it all right, she said, almost whispering. I must have looked surprised.—All right?

—Not all right. But perhaps better than . . . He was dying, she said. Almost matter-of-factly. But not quite.

—What?

—Cancer. He'd known it for weeks. It seemed to change everything for him.

—I can see that. Even if you're eighty . . .

—Eighty-six. He'd always been . . . how should I say it? Serene? Nothing seemed to upset him.

—I guess that's a nice way to be.

—It was as if nothing could really reach him after . . . those years in Baton Rouge, in the legislature.

—When you've fought Huey Long, the rest of life is a cinch.

She smiled that smile again. If someone could talk her into doing a TV commercial, she could sell twenty million of them—whatever they were.

—I hadn't thought of that, but it's true. Then, when he found out about his sickness . . .

—It shook him. Nobody is that . . . serene.

—No. I mean, yes, he was . . . shaken. I can't explain it, but it wasn't knowing he was going to die—not even knowing almost when. It was as if he'd suddenly remembered something he'd forgotten long ago, something terribly important.

—I think I'd feel that way. If I knew I was dying.

—He started going out alone at night. He stopped sitting in the garden with me in the morning, sharing coffee. I'd find him making phone calls, and when he realized I was there, he'd finish and hang up quickly.

Denise had gone through her mason jar by then. With all my baser emotions pounding along, I went to do us both another. She didn't say no. She wasn't even thinking about me or what I was doing. As I mixed, she went on talking, starting to look through one of the scrapbooks.

—He'd never been a terribly religious man. Only Sundays, the holy days, the funeral of a friend, a wedding, a baptism. Then, after he knew how sick he was, he began getting up before dawn. He'd have coffee and then catch the St. Charles trolley down to the cathedral. For early Mass. Sometimes he'd be away all day, into the evening, tell me he'd stopped by the Bethel Bar.

I brought back the mason jars, a dark corner of my mind computing whether I'd try to make her if a half-pint of gin and all that sadness sent her emotions looking for a temporary home. I exited the file, letting the question go on simmering down there.

—Sounds normal to me, I said.—If you're not going to get religious when they tell you you're checking out, you're not going to get religious at all.

Denise sipped her drink and shook her head.—It wasn't that. He wasn't afraid, Mr. Colvin.

—Wes.

—As in John Wesley?

—Not quite. My father had a mean streak. As in John Wesley Hardin.

She nodded as if she understood. Maybe she did.—It was something . . . worse than fear. Something he simply had to get done, something he remembered that was awfully important.

—It's nothing special, I told her.—I've seen it before. When my father was dying, he was compulsive. There was this thing he had to finish . . .

—What?

—Raking the backyard. It was autumn, and the leaves had fallen. It was already cold and he was too weak, so I propped him in a chair in the kitchen where he could look out the window . . .

—You raked the lawn for him.

—I'd always hated to do it before. You'd be surprised how long it can take to clean up every leaf, every piece of leaf, from a half-acre of land. And I didn't work fast. I was . . . very deliberate. Then, deep in the winter that year, I finished and he died.

I know better than to talk about my father. Especially when I've been drinking. Which is almost all the time. He's been dead a dozen years, but that's only time out in the world. Inside, it happens all over again anytime I trip across that not-quite-buried stratum of memory where it's stored.

Denise rose from her chair and looked away. She walked out to the courtyard. The sunlight lay softly on the back wall, bathing each old brick in etching fluid. A mimosa grew in front, close to the house, and its frothy seeds fell onto the shadowed flagstones below, catching a hint of breeze and eddying up again into the light.

—I wish I could have done that for Grand-père, she said.—But what troubled him wasn't as simple as the leaves. I don't suppose I'll ever know what did.

I almost put my arm around her, but something said no. Probably the good redneck peasant blood of my people who know that the touch of an aristocrat is death—in one form or another.

—I'll leave the scrapbooks, she said.—You'll want to go through them. If you need any help, please call.

She had a little pencil with a mother-of-pearl casing hanging around her neck, and she wrote something on the back of a card.

—This is my number, she said.—It's unlisted, but I'm usually there. If I'm not, Carole will take a message. Thanks so much for your time.

I tried to smile back.—I've enjoyed it, I told her. —Maybe next time, it'll be . . . lighter.

—I hope so.

Then she turned to go before she realized she still had the mason jar in her hand.

—Oh . . . I almost took it with me.

—I wouldn't want the police to stop you. Your father would find out you've been slumming.

Denise gave me an odd look. As if it had never occurred to her that I might think something like that.

—What a strange thing to say, she observed. She drained the jar and set it down.—When I think of slums, I think of some people's hearts.

Then we said good-bye and she was gone. I thought I was beginning to understand the deepest motive for revolutions. Peasants like me have no choice. It's the only way we'll ever get the last word—and maybe the aristocrats' women.

CHAPTER
5

I KNEW IT WAS GOING TO BE A LONG EVENING BECAUSE Denise Lemoyne had made it such a short afternoon. I filled my mason jar again, cleared the table I ate off of—on the rare occasions when I ate in—and got the scrapbooks in order.

The first few were nothing important. Snapshots and family portraits of an old established bourgeois New Orleans family back at the turn of the century. There was Auguste Lemoyne on his father's knee, in a lace dress, all of six months old. The photo was in soft tans and browns, faded and still fading. One day, the thickchested man with the bushy mustache and the baby boy with something like a smile on his lips would simply vanish from the square of photo paper backed with cardboard, leaving behind hardly anything more than that mustache and that smile.

There were certificates of achievement and holy pictures from Auguste's first communion and confirmation, a slug from the old *Item* mentioning a piano recital in which he had played. There had been a Liberty Bond rally in late 1917, and Auguste had been part of the band. In fact, he had sung a patriotic song and been part of the tableau.

It went on like that through college, through law school. Auguste Lemoyne had touched every base, turned up in the social columns a decent number of times, attended an inordinate number of parties and tea dances, had left pressed in the pages of one of the scrapbooks a score of boutonnieres that he had worn to Mardi Gras balls during his student years.

Then, just out of law school, he'd joined a prestigious New Orleans firm. It was still in business today, a little of the plush and glitter worn off, but practicing the same kind of law it had fifty years ago: very discreet, very social, very Uptown, very blue-chip. Criminal and divorce work handled only for old clients. It was said that you had to pass a blood test in order for the firm to represent you. It was a color test. The blood had to come out blue. I suspected there might be one other test, and the color for that had to be green.

The clippings and invitations and certificates became monotonous and predictable then. For a couple of years Auguste stayed in the library stacks of the firm working up cases for the senior partners. But there were, it seems, compensations.

In 1925, he'd broken the mold and married a beauty from St. Francisville instead of a local girl. Thérèse Dufour smiled out at me from a wedding picture, then again posed with her delighted husband beside an old car somewhere in City Park. The clipping said that her father was a doctor who held extensive lumber interests in the Bogalusa area and in central Mississippi. Aha. And that's where Auguste had recouped the family fortunes. I smiled back at him. A girl who looked like that, and money too. Maybe that's where the serenity had come from.

Then, almost overnight, the tenor of the clippings changed. It was as if the parties and the holidays and the social rounds had skidded to a stop. The clippings had to do with politics. There were sample ballots and business cards, draft copies of political advertisements, and a poorly printed circular telling of a rally in Gretna supporting Public Service Commissioner Huey P. Long for governor.

I put the book down then. I didn't need it. The rest was going to be simply local color. There was no mystery as to what had happened after that. Auguste Lemoyne had been called to the colors of the Uptown crowd that ran New Orleans. He'd been elected to the legislature in 1928, and had done yeoman service for the big names and bigger money of his class. I'd go through the rest of the scrapbooks tomorrow, slap out a story, pick some of the old photographs to illustrate it with—and set Auguste Lemoyne in his permanent historical niche. I was feeling the gin and a trace of dissatisfaction. Somehow I'd expected more. As if men who take part in great events should be distinguishable from the rest of us who push the days of our lives along like vegetables in a barrow.

For some reason, I reached down and picked up the last of the scrapbooks. Maybe I thought there might be some lead as to the old man's mind in those final years. But when I opened the book and turned the pages, she was everywhere.

What she had felt for her grandfather, he had returned with interest. The final volume of his life was a chronicle of hers. There were photos of Denise as a baby, as a little girl with Auguste and her mother sitting on a lawn in front of some old plantation house. There must have been a score of snapshots of Denise and Auguste in every kind of situation: riding horseback together, at a high-school graduation, side by side, smiling and waving with Sacré Coeur rising in the background. Then a glossy eight-by-ten fell from the book into my lap.

The print was sharp and clear. Denise on her grandfather's arm, serving as queen of his carnival krewe, Pandora, surrounded by other men, each one looking successful and distinguished in his way. I recognized a doctor, Hugh D'Anton, chief of staff at Charity, a bank president—and Henry Holman, the publisher of the *Item*, looking wise, intelligent, humorous. He stood on the other side of Denise, his arm around her as if he had as much right to be as proud as Auguste did.

Denise was radiant, her smile the center of the picture, forcing all the age and knowledge and money to stand as a frame around it. She looked as if she was supremely happy, as if being the make-believe queen of a little-known carnival krewe had been the very summit of her life.

Then, on the last page, there was a picture that stopped me cold. The foreground was overexposed, and there was, as a result, no background at all. It was almost a candid shot, certainly not posed, and probably taken only a short time ago.

Auguste Lemoyne, stooped, hollow-eyed, full of years, his hands holding those of Denise, who stood erect in the glory of her youth and loveliness, head thrown back in laughter. Her fingers were wound tightly in his, and there was passing between them a current of love and admiration that explained why she had said so little about him this afternoon, why she had not wept. The old man's eyes rested upon his lovely granddaughter in such a way as to tell anyone who could see that she, this beautiful, accomplished, remarkable young woman of his blood, was the justification of all his years, their pain, and the meager successes and considerable failures that dog us all down to the grave.

I sat with the scrapbook in my lap for a long while. It made me lonely to see two people so unaffectedly close. If I were less of a realist, I might have wished that Sandy and I had found our way together sooner. But dying doesn't perfect us; it only completes us.

Then the phone rang. It was Jesus, and he was excited.

—I got something. I don't know how far it runs, but . . .

—Where are you? I asked.

—Chart House is where I'm gonna be, he said.—Catch me on the balcony. I got your drink making right now.

It was a fifteen-minute trip, but I took longer. I hadn't

been expecting to go trucking or I would have held back
on the gin. New Orleans cops are funny. Sometimes
they'll can you for an inappropriate laugh. Other times,
they'll let you drive on, plainly afflicted with the blind
staggers. I drove very slowly.

Jesus was where he'd said he'd be. It was dark by
then, and he stood out like a ghost in his white suit there
on the balcony at a tiny table between two shrubs. I
joined him, and sat down. He wanted to start in before
they got my drink on the table, but I shook my head and
looked toward the street a floor below. From the balcony of the Chart House we could look down into the
muted lights and shadowed trees of Jackson Square. Out
beyond, I could see a freighter moving downriver toward the Gulf, its lights twinkling like hedgehopping
stars.

—You ask around, you pick up shit, Jesus said. His
eyes were bright, and his nerves were like stretched
wire. I knew he had something.

—You know Lupo Dupre? Naw, you don't know Lupo.
You too square. Lupo does big drugs. His old man left
him a grocery store in Gentilly. He moves shit with all
kinds of broke-down people. People cops never look at.
He talked to this old lady . . .

Her name was Helen Lane, and she was forcibly
retired from whoring because of the onset of advancing
old age and a loathsome disease. She lived in a little
apartment on Governor Nicholls Street deeper in the
Quarter. Once in a while she moved some cocaine around
town for Lupo. Sometimes she did a little stock shelving
for people, a little cleaning to bring in another twenty
now and then. One of the places she worked was in a
camera store. The one right next to the Bethel Bar.

—She was finishing up. No, she was already finished.
She was locking the front door and turning away when
she saw him coming down the street.

—Who?

—Man, you not gonna believe it.

—Not if you don't tell me.

—Helen said he looked crazy. Had on a raincoat with

both hands inside it. Like he was carrying something, trying to keep it from getting wet. He went into the Bethel . . .

—Who?

—She knew him. She felt like he was bad trouble, but what do you do? You call the cops on account of how you feel? Shit, they'll whip up on you, take *you* in.

—Goddamnit to hell, who?

—Grubbs.

—That's bullshit. You tell your old whore her eyes are gone.

—Aw, man . . .

—Jesus, he's in. They paroled him five or six months ago. Then they picked him up for doing T's and blues. He's in Charity, and when they find him and drag him back up out of his own asshole, they're gonna revoke the parole and ship him back.

—She knew the bastard. He used to hang around the bar.

—Sure. Because Sandy worked there, and he was married to Sandy. But that was years ago. He's still in the nut box down at Charity.

—Helen says no. She told me what she saw.

—They got room for Helen down at Charity, too.

—Man, you so full of shit. I mean, what kind of reporter are you?

—You want to get Rat in on it?

—No. I want me and you to be in on it. 'Cause if I find out he did it, you got to call Carazo Colón to make some big bail for me.

—You got something like an address?

—Lupo said where he was staying. Grubbs used to do stuff for Lupo. Little chickenshit stuff. Lupo never trusted him.

—Lupo's smart.

—You gonna drink that drink?

I was playing tourist, looking down Decatur toward the business district, over at the sparkling mass of the Jackson Brewery. I was thinking. A bad notion crossed my mind. I decided I'd be better off talking.

—Yeah, I'm going to drink it. I wasn't going to because I've been drinking all afternoon, but now I am.

—What the fuck's with you, man? I never seen you this way. I mean, like if Grubbs . . .

Jesus shifted nervously in his chair just as my eyes came back to him. I caught a glimpse of a pistol in his belt.

—Aha.

—Aha your ass, he said, following my eyes.—What did you think? I'm gonna go down to Criminal Court and watch 'em try him? Give him another fiver and then turn him loose? Oh no, sweet man. We gonna talk, we gonna tell and . . .

—Two-for-one sale. When the smoke clears, Rat gets his corpse and your cock. And when they drop you in the slam, they'll never turn you loose. You'll do twenty. Everybody hates greasers.

It didn't bring Jesus down. His hands still looked like claws, and his eyes were bouncing around like pinballs in his face. But thinking on Grubbs made him meditative. You ask how a man can be at the blurred edge of berserk and meditative at the same time? How do I know? Jesus was full of otherworldly qualities.

—You know what I got to do. I never picked it. I never said, Hey, somebody bump my brother and here I come.

I knew what he was saying, and I agreed with him. It's what I'd do. I hope. If I had a brother. Even cold sober, that's how I think. You let the little things pass. You don't throw your life away for nothing. But big things can't pass. They won't pass. If somebody rapes and kills your daughter or murders your brother in cold blood, and you pass up a clear chance at him, don't kid yourself. You're not a law-abiding citizen. You're garbage.

—Okay, I said.—It just took me a few minutes to get in the mood.

Jesus smiled, reached over and patted my hand. God knows why he took me so seriously, why my benediction mattered to him. But it did, and usually I tried to be careful with it. This was not a time to be careful. If he was right. If Helen Lane wasn't letting her tertiary syphilis bugs talk for her.

I had come across Lester Grubbs just once. When some collection of retardates they called the Pardon and Parole Board had put him back on the street. Somehow, in the dim fluid recesses of whatever sloshed around in his head in place of a brain, Lester had the notion that Sandy had been waiting for him, that life had been insupportable for her while he was in stir—despite the fact that he'd shot at her and she'd divorced him as fast as the law allowed. Lester seemed to live in his own head. I began to realize what Denise's last remark had meant. I hoped it didn't apply to me, but God knows Lester Grubbs lived in a slum.

Jesus insisted on paying the tab, and we went downstairs and started walking toward the address he'd gotten from Lupo. Neither of us felt like talking. Nightfall hadn't done a thing for the heat. I was sweating under my jacket and thinking what a dumb idea this was. Just suppose Grubbs was the man. If he was, we were casually walking toward an encounter with a guy who had himself an automatic weapon and didn't mind wasting a dozen people plus one. For whatever reason. And who had better than good reason to blow me away on sight.

Jesus had a .38 special in his belt which he might or might not know how to use. Me? I had my teeth and nails. Maybe I should pick up a beer bottle out of a trash can, break off the bottom, and be prepared. You can commit atrocities with a broken beer bottle. Unless the other guy has something better. Like a MAC-10.

Sandy and I had been talking the afternoon Lester had turned up. I was sitting at the bar. She was behind it mixing something like a hurricane for some tourist who'd accidentally wandered in. I saw her face go white—not so much with fear as dismay. Then Lester appeared in the mirror and sat down on a barstool one away from mine. He was scrawny and looked undernourished. He was wearing a baseball cap over long ill-cut hair that was going from a washed-out blond to a chalky white with no pause in between.

He was so deeply suntanned—or burned—that when I first saw him, I thought he was a black who'd gone utterly crackers and dyed his hair a color that made no sense at all. But no. Lester had picked up his California beachboy-plus look the old-fashioned way. He'd been chopping cotton up at Angola with his peers for the past couple of seasons. Till the simians on Pardons and Paroles decided in one of their usual fits of reefer madness to turn him loose on the public once more. For chuckles.

—This is the first place they're gonna look for you, Sandy had said, still working on the hurricane. She couldn't manage to keep her hands from trembling.

—Naw, Lester said.—They ain't looking for me at all. I'm paroled.

—Holy shit, Sandy said.—What for?

—Good time, sugar buns, good time. I done right up there for two years, and they done forgive the rest. So long as I keep straight and check in with Mr. Denzil once a week.

—That's swell.

—Now you and me got to talk.

—No we don't.

—I don't want to hear that. I done paid what I owed.

—Not to me you haven't, you miserable sonofabitch.

That struck Lester wrong. He reached over and knocked the hurricane glass out of Sandy's hands. I started to move, but she glanced at me, and I held.

—Lester, she said.—Hit the road. Unless you want to go back to chopping cotton for another couple of years.

—Listen, all I thought about up there was you.

—You wasted your time.

—Bullshit. You thought about me.

—Not once. You never crossed my mind.

That made Lester look evil. For just a moment, he wanted to kill her. You didn't need an abnormal psychology textbook to see that. After he got himself settled inside, he looked over at me.

—You been fooling with my woman, ain't you?

I just stared back at him, wondering what he had under his dirty jeans-jacket, how fast he could move,

and what I was going to do about it. He looked in a hell
of a lot better condition than I was. I figured he could
move pretty fast.

—You're fixing to blow it, Sandy said wearily. I reckoned there was no need for me to get upset until I heard
some fear in her voice.

—Was you waiting around till I got sent up? Or did
you come sniffing her out after I was gone?

Lester seemed to have a talent for asking questions
that no one could answer. Maybe that was a symptom of
his trouble. Maybe he just wasn't meant for this world.
What can you do with a man who always asks questions
no one can answer? We stared at each other for what
seemed to me a long, long time. Sandy was mixing
another drink, keeping her eyes on both of us. After
enough of it, Lester seemed satisfied.

—Tell you what, he said smoothly.—I'm gonna let it
go. What the shit? You get up and move on out, and I'm
gonna forget I ever seen you. This here's mine. You go
get your own pussy out on the street, hear? Lord, it's all
over the place.

—Goddamn, Sandy said, as I got off my stool. Then
she threw the drink she was mixing in Lester's face.
Which kept him from seeing me pick up my barstool. I
think he got his eyes clear just in time to see me heft the
stool and bring it down on his head as hard as I could.

They came and took Lester away and patched him up
at Charity. When they checked out his pockets, they
found some street drugs on him. That was the last anybody had heard of him until now. I liked to think that
Lester was, at bottom, chickenshit. Most of us are. If
the streets and houses of New Orleans or any other
town were peopled with Jim Bowies and Bedford For-
rests, human society would be impossible. It was important for me to believe Lester didn't really want to go to
the mat for the last showdown, because if he did, it was
sure I'd be a prime target. And nobody could be easier
to take out.

The truth was, I'd never thought of Lester in connection with the killings at Bethel. But that was because I

thought he was in Charity, that they had him down for the count.

Now, as Jesus and I moved through the dark streets, both of us sweating our private memories, our own motives for the walk, I wondered whether Lester had been biding his time, waiting for some certain moment to even the score. But then, if he'd been willing to wipe out the Bethel Bar to get the equation in balance, why hadn't he waited for me?

Could it have been Lester who called? I tried to remember his voice, but it blurred and merged with the voices of every truck driver and short-order cook and fishing-camp owner I'd ever heard back home. Or what if he'd had someone call? Maybe the great sorrow of Lester's life had been walking into the Bethel Bar, throwing open his raincoat for the Great Announcement, and realizing, even as he pulled the trigger and watched that world dissolve into splinters and shards and chunks of wood and glass and flesh and bone, that I wasn't there. That the scales were still tipped to the measure of a barstool across the head.

—Okay, Jesus said, catching my arm.—This is it.

It was a big dark house, three stories at least. It loomed out of the shadows like the superstructure of an old battleship, a round tower at one end with a roof like an inverted funnel at the top. I could see only a single soft faded light far down the front hallway behind a door with burglar bars and full-length decorative glass behind.

—Where the hell are we? I asked Jesus.

—Esplanade, he said.—Why?

I didn't realize how far we'd walked. My mind had been on other things. Getting there swept away the probing in motives and reveries. I could feel the late-summer heat against my body, but I was cold.

—You got anything for me? I asked Jesus.

He smiled, laughed softly.—Thought you wasn't going to ask.

He reached in his white coat pocket and handed me something small enough to hide in my hand. It was a .25 Beretta automatic. Nickel-plated. A woman's purse gun.

No doubt you could kill a man with it, but medical school training would help. I had never known of anyone killed with a .25. What I did remember was a vice cop who'd had to use the .25 he carried strapped to his leg as a hideout. He'd emptied it into a pimp—seven shots. After that, the pimp had broken the cop's leg, given him a fractured skull, and walked away.

—What am I supposed to do? Throw it at him?

—Whatever's right, man. You throw better than you shoot?

We walked up to the door. I was about to ring what looked like a broken doorbell. Jesus pulled my hand away.

—You mind if we sneak up on him? he said.—I ain't gonna duel the sonofabitch. I got bushwhacking in mind.

—Like you say. Whatever's right.

The door pushed open at his touch, and I realized we were inside one of those grand old derelicts on Esplanade that dated from the nineteenth century, when it was one hell of a street. Now the place was chopped into apartments—five, six, maybe ten of them. I smelled chili oil and some kind of fish frying. It was quiet, but at the lower threshold of hearing, somebody behind one of those closed doors was rattling away in Spanish.

—Forget it, Jesus told me.—He's just telling her to give him the money or he'll cut her throat.

—That's not Grubbs. He'd cut her throat and take the money. Anyhow, the dumb fuck can't even talk English.

Jesus motioned me to stay where I was. He went down the long hall beside the stairway and slapped one of the doors. After a moment, someone answered, but the light was bad, and Jesus blocked off the doorway. Whoever came said something in Spanish, and Jesus replied. It went back and forth between them for a moment, and I looked up the long shadowy staircase.

The banisters were worn and chipped, painted and repainted, but I could see that the place had once been beautiful. The walls were cracked plaster with peeling latex paint down to a chair rail of raised hardwood. Below, under layers of paint on the paneling, I could

still make out the elaborate design of leaves carved out
in lacy curves. Up above the single dangling bulb strung
from a frazzled wire, there was an ornate broken plaster
medallion fixed to the ceiling.

I found myself wondering about the people who had
lived here when the place was new. Then I flushed that
out, and checked the automatic. The clip was full, and I
levered one into the chamber. Right upper center body,
five rounds and pause, I thought. It's always good to
have a plan, so long as you know they never work past
the first fifteen milliseconds. If they did, I'd have been
the toughest honcho in Shreveport.

Just then, the tone changed down the dim hall where
Jesus and his newfound *compadre* were talking. As I
shifted my eyes, I saw Jesus come out of his belt with an
old S & W .38 that looked the size of a leg of lamb. He
seemed to be pushing it up somebody's nose, and then I
heard:

—*Veinte y tres, veinte y tres. Señor, no me . . .*

—*Veinte y tres . . .?*

—*Sí, sí . . . por supuesto . . .*

Jesus turned, the door slammed shut, and the S & W
seemed to be floating down the hall unaided. Pointed
toward my belly. It was nickel-plated, too. Jesus seemed
to feel that was the only way to go with ordnance.

—Okay, we're on. Second floor. Room . . .

—Twenty-three.

—You speak Spanish?

—Shit, Jesus . . .

—Come on . . .

We started up the stairway then, Jesus determined to
go on ahead, and me happy to see him with so much
initiative. We paused on the landing and listened. Nothing. I have no idea what we would have done if we'd
heard something. Like someone drawing the bolt on that
damned submachine gun that I could almost see, having
never seen.

Up there, at the top of the stairs, it was pitch dark.
No light at all.

—What'd that guy tell you? I asked Jesus

—Nothing.

—Horseshit. He gave you the number. Anyhow, you were banging along with him for a couple of minutes.

—He said the light up here was burned out. The fucking landlord won't spring for a dollar fifty. Somebody is gonna break his neck sooner or later.

—What do you say we wait here and watch Grubbs come out and break his neck. That way, everybody gets what he wants. Free. Even the fucking landlord.

Jesus had to laugh.—You know, he said casually, —when we go back to retake the motherland, I don't think I want you along.

—That hurts, I told him.—But whatever you say.

We inched up the stairs into the shadows slowly, waiting for our eyes to adjust. Once we made the top, it wasn't that bad. The hall was wide, larger than most rooms in a modern house. I could see four doors, two on either side. There was a large double window at the end of the hall that looked down over the street. From out there, the least bit of bluish light illumined the place. There was an armoire between the doors against one wall, and a long low chest against the other. Down at the far end, beneath the window, I could see a table and a few chairs scattered here and there. Jesus pointed with the S & W to the first door on the left.

—Somebody cover, somebody kick down the door, he said tensely.

That's how they do it on TV, right? Still, it seemed to me there was a problem.

—What you gonna do? Jesus asked, anxious to get it on.

—I think I'm going to check the door, I told him.

Because I suspected that they still had the old doors in place. And I reckoned if they did, we could both kick for the next hour and a half and not even budge that one in front of us. It would be made of oak through and through, most likely, and you don't kick them down like you slap aside a hollow-core veneer door.

I moved close, squinted. Sure enough. The door was divided into panels. It was as solid as the doorframe.

But before I could turn and tell Jesus that there had to be another way, I noticed a thin slit of light at the edge of the door where the knob was. A line of flickering blue light coming from inside. The dumb bastard hadn't even closed the door—much less locked it. I pointed out the light to Jesus. He nodded. Okay, if we were going to do it, we ought to get to doing it.

I started to push the door open slowly, but Jesus shook his head and shoved me aside. He backed up a few feet, and then, before I could suggest any tactics, he ran at it full tilt.

It wasn't because I was lagging, but because for just some fraction of a second I couldn't believe what he was doing, that I was still in the hallway when that single shot, louder than a tank gun, boomed through the hollows of the old house and began sending its reverberations back at me before I could get off the dime and throw myself into the room behind him.

CHAPTER
6

T HAT FRACTION OF A SECOND HAD COST ME. IT WAS ALL
over when I got myself through the door. Jesus
stood, a puzzled look on his face, the big ugly S & W
hanging from his hand, smoke, believe it or not, curling
from the muzzle.

As for Lester Grubbs, his worrying days were over.
He was going to be free for the rest of time—unless he
was reincarnated as a cockroach—and the rest of us
were going to be free of him.

He sat in a heavy, ragged overstuffed chair directly
across from a portable TV turned to "Music Television,"
the sound turned off. He held his submachine gun
stretched across his legs, right hand in place, finger on
trigger. Lester's eyes were squinted almost to closing as
he peered intently at some girl with a crew cut in a Nazi
SS uniform climbing out of a black egg stretched across
a midnight blue sky. My first thought was, Jesus didn't
move that fast. Lester must have lost his edge. Then I

noticed the middling-sized hole directly between Lester's eyes.

—When I saw that piece of his, Jesus began.

—Right. Hello, Lester. We got to talk. See if this won't loosen you up. Christ, Jesus, you nailed him square between the eyes.

—Listen, man, you think I should of talked to him about it?

—I'm on your side, I told him.—Only trouble is, it's gonna be tough to interrogate him.

I was looking at Lester as we talked, thinking that something just wasn't right. Then it hit me. Lester did indeed have a righteous hole consistent with the through-and-through passage of a flat-nosed, wadcutter, .38 special slug right above the bridge of his nose. But it wasn't bleeding. No blood at all. Wait, back up. Some trifle of dark blood at the very edges of the entry wound. Much slush on the chair behind, and a line of what my buddies at the coroner's office call biological matter on the floor back of the chair. But nothing like those folks I'd seen in the Bethel Bar. None running down his face like thick tears. I reached over and tried to turn his face into the light. He was stiff as a board.

—Fuck, man. You acting like I did wrong.

—Never that, Jesus. The truth is, I don't think you've done anything at all.

—What?

—I think you shot a dead man.

Jesus looked at me for the first time. He shivered. —That's sick, man. I don't do nothing to dead people. The sonofabitch was coming up with that thing on his lap. Then I . . .

I wasn't paying a lot of attention. I was looking around the room. Lester didn't care, and I didn't need a search warrant because I wasn't a cop. On a table near a window, there was a loaf of moldy Bunny bread and a jar of peanut butter without a lid. Right next to it was a moderately nice example of what they call riding tackle—a heroin shoot-up kit with an alcohol lamp, a spoon, a loop of rubber tubing, some cheap packaged syringes, and two or three packets of white powder. One of the packets was open, and I dipped a finger in. Not powdered milk, granulated sugar, or Sweet'n Low. Why was I doing this? I thought. I hadn't the faintest idea what heroin tasted like. It could be plaster of paris for all I knew. But Jesus had shaken himself out of his funk, walked over by the table, and was watching me now, waiting for some kind of a verdict.

—Heavy, I said, for no reason I could think of.

Jesus dipped his finger into the stuff. He hadn't learned his moves from *The French Connection*. Ignacio had taught him. Back in the old days when you made your first stake off a collection of zombies who were so far gone in the junk that it was hard to feel anything wrong about selling it at all.

—Wow, he said, shaking his head.—Wait till the narcs get hold of this.

—What? I said.

—You said it was heavy. You know what I know, Jesus told me, one expert to another.

—Right, I said, my last claim to honesty and character—if I still had one—glimmering away.

—Who you think peddles this stuff? I could flame out half the heads in the Quarter with one bag.

—You want to call and see if we can roust out Rat?

Jesus looked grim.—Man, I don't know. How do you feel about a animous call?

—What?

—You know . . . Where you call and tell and don't say who. Like that call you got.

Anonymous. Right. I considered it. I'd just as soon Rat Trapp didn't think we were both nuts, or setting up our own police department. Rat had no time for amateurs at all. Not because he had any objection to cowboy justice, but because even a self-respecting vigilante committee or lynch mob has got to have certain standards. I was dead sure Jesus and I couldn't make the cut.

—Look, we got to do it that way, Jesus said.—Rat's gonna shit when he sees . . .

—That some loony dorked a dead man? He'll understand, I said ironically.

We decided to meet the mess head-on. I stayed by the
foot of the stairs while Jesus beat on the door of his
amigo at the back of the hall. There was another intense
whispered discussion back there. My Spanish edges up
to nothing, but I think Jesus told the guy he'd just blown
the brains out of one hombre and would as soon make it
a pair. It was quiet for a moment, then the guy invited
Jesus in to use his phone. My house is your house.

I got Jesus to phone Bob Pleasance, too. I couldn't
bat out a story till we had something more to go with,
but we had enough to suggest that Lester was a good
solid suspect. Even in New Orleans, every hood doesn't
carry a MAC–10. At least not yet. We had Helen Lane,
we had the submachine gun, we had enough dope to
infer that Lester had levitated down to the Bethel Bar in
one of his run-of-the-mill horse-powered ugly moods.
We had Sandy's divorcing him for what passes as motive—and we had what was left of Lester. He hadn't
died from Jesus' shot, and I doubted it was heart or liver
failure. Jesus, grinning from ear to ear, came back out of
his amigo's pad, the door slamming shut fast behind
him.

—What? I asked.

—Cops coming. Rat on his way.

—How about Pleasance? Did you get him?

—Yeah, man. Sure.

—What'd you say?

—I told him, Stop the Presses . . .

He did. Later, Pleasance would ask me what kind of
dipshits I was hanging around with and using for sources.
Stop the presses? Holy Christ.

Never mind. The presses, such as they are, kept right
on running. But Pleasance was on notice that I might
need a hole on the front page for the late editions.

While we waited, Jesus ran down the hall and beat on
the door again. He came back with a bottle of tequila, a
packet of salt, and two jelly glasses. We drank.

—How do you know that beano back there's not

going to tell the cops you broke in, assaulted him, and stole the booze.

—Oh, man, you really think bad of Latin people.

—Bullshit. You're not Latin. *Omnia gallinas divisa est in partes tres* . . . and parts is parts.

He just stared at me and licked the salt off his hand as he dropped another shot of the tequila.—I told him I was a narc. Did he want me to get a warrant? Shit no, he didn't want me to get no warrant.

—*Omnes greasers narcoti est* . . .

—The man is from Chihuahua. He got him a stash of different things. For religious purposes.

—Aha. A Catholic.

—Yeah. No lousy *protestante*. Big balls. Lots of kids.

That's what passed for communication between us. When nothing was happening, we just flogged along, insulting one another's heritage. We both meant it, but it didn't mean anything. I think we both understood that the heritage is gone, that losing it sooner or later is the unmentioned price of admission into the USA.

I had been juiced before all this began, but the walk and the business at the door had generated some powerful and sobering hormones. Now the tequila, which I do not like, was easing me back down again.

—I think my fucking brother died of an accident, Jesus said, his voice low, infinitely sad.

—I got to believe somebody did, I answered.

—You think that shit upstairs really did what he did to get even with Sandy?

I didn't say anything for a while. My first thought was, no way. She hadn't been cheating on him. He hadn't ever really given a damn about her. They'd crossed paths, gotten married the way most people do, and when it went bad, they'd gone their ways. What's to shoot about? On the other hand, Lester didn't have much experience contemplating the meaning and ethics of situations. Maybe he did do it for that. Or maybe he expected me to be there.

—It doesn't matter, I told Jesus.

Jesus nodded, but he wasn't letting it go.—Maybe he had a tumor in his brain.

—No room. Maybe he had the red-ass. I busted a barstool over his head awhile back. Before they picked him up.

—Hey, yeah. Why was he out?

—Don't ask me. There's this Pardon and Parole Board. They let everybody out. Nothing you can do about it. The system puts them in for killing or robbing, and the board lets them out. That's how they play the game in Louisiana.

—Maybe we hire a hit on the board.

I turned to him and took the tequila one last time. —You know, that's a good idea. Who could we get?

Jesus shrugged.—Felipe Taugaun. He used to do really bad stuff in Mexico. *Federale.* Worked off-days for the PRI. Shot students.

—How the fuck did he get into the country?

—Hey, man, how you think? He walked. Just like everybody else.

Just then, the police showed. Three cars. Guns drawn. One tall black cop with a sawed-off shotgun, and a couple of white guys who looked like they'd vacationed in Sicily. Hell, I thought, they all want to be in the Marines. They want to hit a place and walk away leaving ninety-seven-percent casualties behind. This is bad for law and order.

They were all right, though, when they found out that Lester was nonviolent. Jesus and I had tucked away our armament and sat watching the cops rig an emergency light in the upper hallway and stand around looking vigilant till Rat turned up.

He looked fine, really fine. Pearl gray suit, dark blue tie on an off-white shirt. I always wondered where he went dressed like that. The only place I could think of that fit was the sunken bar at Restaurant Jonathan, the Art Deco capital of the Deep South.

—Well, well, he said, looking at us without any humor at all.—Here's the Inter-American Bilingual Crime-fighters League. What you two motherfuckers been up to?

We shrugged and nodded up the stairs. The first wave of cops was standing firm. Probably almost nothing had been stolen from Lester's room since they arrived. Rat went up, and five minutes later, here came the coroner's people and all those forensic and Criminal Investigation Division types. Same people I'd seen at the Bethel Bar. They stared at Jesus and me; we stared back at them.

—See, Jesus said.—They're not used to seeing newspaper people where shit goes down. They looking for the TV.

—Me too.

After fifteen minutes or so, Rat sent for us.

—Okay, he said.—This is just how it was when youall found him by a process of shrewd deduction?

Jesus looked uncertain. I looked fine.—Right, I said.

—Which one of you turkey-asses mutilated the body?

—*Dios*, Jesus said, turning a nice mauve under the police emergency lights.

—What? I asked.

—Look, Rat said in a fractious tone,—I was at a reunion of the 331st Military Police Unit when they called me out. There was this woman had her hand on my leg telling me how she felt about fighting men. Now I'm here, and I'm pissed. I want to know who come in this room so low-down mean drunk he had to shoot up a corpse.

We explained the thing to him. No, I did. Jesus just nodded. Rat held out his hand for the gun. Jesus handed it to him. He looked at me coldly.—Are the slugs from this hog leg gonna match the one we pulled from the chair?

—It'd better, I said.

—Amen, Rat replied.

—Are the bullets you pulled from those folks at the bar going to match that Uzi or whatever it is? I asked him.

He nodded.—MAC–10, just like I told you. You ain't gonna get a bet against it from me. It's the right caliber and the right model. What about Lester Grubbs here?

I told him what I knew. His eyes widened when I said

Lester had been in for drug abuse, that he was supposed
to be having a hearing for parole violation when they
cleaned him up enough at Charity to tune in on the
material world.

—Is that so?

—Check it out.

—Oh, you know it, honey.

It started winding down then. Rat told Jesus to hit the
road and dragged me with him down to his car. We
started driving.

—Neck bones? I asked.—What about oxtails?

—Too late. We ought to be in bed. I had two things.
One is, thanks. Even if you and that pachuco are born
fuck-ups, you look to have come up with the right boy.

—You think so?

—We'll know in the morning. If we got the gun, we
just got to have the man.

—And something like a motive.

—Ah, Rat said, looking straight ahead as we drove
toward East New Orleans.—Yeah . . .

—No?

—I never said that. People do stuff like that. I remember reading about that dude in the Texas tower while I
was in service. When I was a kid, some drunk old fool
got pushed off a Desire trolley by the white conductor
for making a fuss. Had him an old grenade from the war
at home. Tossed it on the next trolley passed.

—Shit . . .

—I asked him why he didn't at least wait for the same
trolley to come back around. Said he was tired and
didn't have time. Had to get up early for work.

—Did he . . .

—Killed four people. Seeing what I've seen, you
couldn't hardly give me a motive I wouldn't check out.
Yeah, Lester could of done it. He had enough reason.
For him.

We stopped at some black bar out off Forstall Avenue, and I went back to gin and tonic one more time.
What the hell? Pleasance had put me on leave, as it

were. And I'd had a bad couple of days. Then Rat took me back to my car.

—The other thing, he said.—Reckon you could hold on writing up Lester till I get ballistics and a couple other things?

—How long? I said.—All those network freaks and wire people are gonna get wind of it.

Rat looked pained.—You know better than that. Do like I say, and I'll hand you a package. Give you one-edition lead. Is that good enough?

—I believe it is. Between friends.

He smiled and reached out his hand. I took it.

—You're not going to worry about Jesus being fast on the draw, are you?

Rat laughed.—Shit, if I'd of gone in that door and saw what he did, old Lester wouldn't of had no head at all. You got a suspect with a lap full of iron like that, color him dead, man. Naw, if the slug checks with Jesus' piece, we'll just drop the hole in Lester's head out of the report.

Then an idea struck him. He cackled.—How about we say he already had that hole in his head, always had it? That's what made him so goddamned mean.

We both laughed. I got out and drove home. It looked like all the excitement was over. Tomorrow would be dawning cool and turning hot. There was a sixty-percent chance of thundershowers in the afternoon. Pleasance would be hassling me as to why I went along on holding the Grubbs story. I wouldn't even bother answering. He'd know why.

As I killed the lights and lay down to sleep, there was only one thing that still didn't set right. One question I didn't have an answer for—at least none that seemed more probable than not.

What about that phone call? Had the caller died at Bethel? Or had he called on behalf of Lester Grubbs to set me up? And either way, what the hell was a deduction box?

CHAPTER
7

I DON'T KNOW HOW I DO IT, BUT THE NEXT MORNING I woke up just before the sun, and the headache and rigors of the gut were only passing bad. I drank my coffee and got back on the scrapbooks, moving through them quickly, noticing that Auguste had dropped out of the Comus carnival krewe in 1936 and helped to found Pandora. Small club. No parade. Just a banquet and a formal dance during Mardi Gras every year. Such a change seemed odd, but who knows what kind of idiocy passes current between people in high society? Maybe Mrs. DeBug had made an upleasant remark about Mrs. Lemoyne's gown, and that had torn it with Comus.

The only thing worth noting was that Pandora seemed to have a pretty solid membership. As the picture I'd seen the night before indicated, Henry Holman, the *Item* publisher, was a member. In fact, as I looked down the list of founding members on that faded, brown-edged, foxed original invitation, I saw a number of names I recognized.

When I got done with the last of the scrapbooks and spent a few minutes looking lovingly at the photos of Denise at play, in tennis togs, bathing suits, party dresses, I started to work on my feature about Auguste Lemoyne. The first part just fell into the word processor without any thinking required.

I got well into the second part, put young Auguste into the Louisiana legislature as a champion of the rights of conservative old New Orleans against the populist hordes that Huey and his boys were raising up, and then I stopped.

I laughed and put some fresh water on to boil. I really did need to see Denise again. Not simply to trace her grandfather's motivations in those early days, but to get a clean, clear setting of the time and what was at stake. If she'd done a senior thesis on those days, she had to be as good a source as I could find. That made me feel good. I wouldn't have to lie. It could go on being business. For a while. Till I could tell if there was anything else.

They were burying Auguste Lemoyne out of St. Louis Cathedral that morning, according to the paper. It wasn't his religious parish, but there had been some kind of dispensation. Long ago, Auguste Lemoyne had lived in the Quarter, and one of his oldest friends was Father John Cunningham.

The priest was associated with the cathedral in some way, and I'd seen him on page after page of the old scrapbooks. At Auguste's wedding, as an usher, before he'd entered the seminary; up in Baton Rouge with Auguste during the school textbook battle in Huey's first year as governor (he and Auguste almost surely on opposite sides at least that once); at the cathedral baptizing Denise, a tiny overdressed confection of silk and lace in her mother's arms (Drew Lemoyne standing nearby, but behind Auguste, somehow detached from the family scene, less involved with his new daughter than was his father). There was even an old photo of the priest with the founding members of Pandora back in 1936.

A shower, along with a can of V-8, and feeling my way slowly into a suit and tie reminded me of my humanity. Maybe, after the funeral service, I'd stay in the Quarter, stand in line outside Galatoire's, and have a fine lunch. One beer only. I'd have to check in at the city room later, and then find out what Rat had. After that, a decent interval having passed, maybe I could call Denise and finish working up the last part of my feature on the old man.

It was still cool outside when I drove to the Quarter and parked. The walk to St. Louis Cathedral was pleasant. In an hour or so, it wouldn't be. By the time the funeral Mass was done, the streets would be blazing, the humidity up close to saturation. As I reached Jackson Square, I looked up. The sky was full of white fluffy clouds shifting, changing form. Toward their center, they were darkening to gray. That was because they were thunderheads, soaring, building up to forty thousand feet above. Auguste would likely take his last ride in the rain. Out to a marble niche in the Lemoyne tomb I'd seen pictured in the scrapbooks, in a snapshot of Auguste and a young Denise there on some All Souls' Day years ago. He was still vigorous, she small and adorable. They had been tending a tomb that resembled a small classical temple in size and shape. Except, perched oddly, asymmetrically, on one side of the roof, was the blank white statue of an angel weeping. Burial conventions aside, what could reduce an angel to tears?

St. Louis Cathedral is in a class by itself. Take away the ornate altar, and it could be a Protestant church built during the baroque. Despite all its popish flummery, plaster statues, and overreaching painted motifs, it is austere, chaste, a masterpiece of design and grace. If I were God, I'd stay there a lot.

The church was almost full, but I wasn't looking for a seat. I edged my way up the right aisle and stood at the corner of the apse along with what I took to be a huddling of ordinary people who had known Auguste

Lemoyne in one capacity or another. Some of the women were sobbing into handkerchiefs. All of them were looking sad and depressed. Not as if they were saying good-bye to a man who had lived his fair share of years and a few more, but as if they had lost someone who still mattered in their lives.

In the family pew, I saw Drew and Denise, and a few old folks I didn't know. In the pew just behind, there sat Henry Holman. On either side of him were men of varying ages, some no older than I, some ancient. They sat upright, looking straight ahead—not at the dark wood casket surrounded by flowers. They seemed more than a chance gathering of men at a funeral. There was a solidarity, a community between them—as you might see in a group of military officers sitting side by side in plain clothes at a civilian social gathering.

I was watching Denise, but I couldn't help noticing that Drew Lemoyne had his eyes on a side altar as the Mass began. He wasn't glancing at it. He was studying it. I followed his eyes. It was a simple marble altar with a tabernacle at the back, and a statue of Jesus on a pedestal above. Nothing special about it: a traditional Catholic thing with Christ's chest bared, robes pulled aside to reveal his red heart surrounded by a circle of thorns, topped with a small flame.

Father Cunningham gave a eulogy that should send any man content to that long sleep. Maybe half the congregation dozed off, too. Not me. I was listening. Cunningham had known Auguste Lemoyne most of his life. Making allowances for his pulpit rhetoric, maybe I could catch that tone of déjà vu I wanted for the feature.

The old priest made something of a hero out of his friend. It dawned on me that I'd never heard the anti-Long side of things set out passionately. Father Cunningham took care of that deficit for me. He painted Huey as a buffoon, a crude country man motivated, driven, by one of the seven deadly sins: envy. Huey had despised New Orleans precisely because it represented all the facets of life that he lacked the capacity to value, to enjoy. It is a terrible thing for a man to set himself to destroying what he does not understand, cannot appreciate.

Auguste, on the other hand, had worn his honored old family name lightly, always ready to assist those less fortunate. He had been dedicated to the culture that had given him life and purpose. He had been deeply religious. He and Huey Long illustrated the extremes of human possibility. Auguste was surely at peace now. The good priest made no speculation as to Huey's situation.

When the Mass was done, the mourners began passing by the casket slowly, some pausing, reaching out to touch one of their own. I have never liked the practice of open coffins, but good people differ on the point. For some reason, this time I felt that I should join the file, walk by and pay something like last respects to the old man. Was it because I was in the process of putting together the nearest thing to a historical judgment that Auguste Lemoyne was likely to get? Or because mine had been the first human hand to touch him kindly after Lester Grubbs had blasted the life out of him and all his momentary neighbors at the Bethel Bar?

When I reached the coffin, I must have gasped. The old lady ahead of me turned, gave me a sharp look. I pretended to be coughing into my hand.

Had someone asked me on oath to identify the body lying there, to state that he was the very one I had found dead in a booth at Bethel, I couldn't have done it. No way to know how much my uncertainty arose from the undertaker's art, how much the fact that as we reach great age, many of us lose our individuality and become one, merged together in that figure, Old Man.

But beyond that, Auguste Lemoyne lay with a rosary twisted around his hands, crucifix in his fingers. And he was wearing the hooded brown habit of a Franciscan monk.

I must have stared for a moment too long because I felt someone's elbow jab me from behind. I moved on, and kept walking, making a little detour through the pews so that I could leave by the side exit and not wait

in the line of those who were giving condolences to
Denise and Drew and the other anonymous family members at the main door. They were getting enough of
those. They didn't need mine.

But in the shadowy vestibule I paused and looked
over at Denise, who stood dressed in black with a short
veil, shaking hands, nodding as old men and women
rattled on to her, each one saying what Auguste had
meant to them, or passing on some anecdote, something
he had said or done that only they knew. Once, as a
matron passed on out of the church and another ap-
proached her, she looked up in my direction, her green
eyes flat and dark and doubly veiled. I doubted that she
saw me or recognized me, and I walked outside into the
light.

Jesus wasn't at his shop. I understood that. He was
probably wrecked from the night before. Anyhow, there
was nothing either of us had to do, so it didn't matter. I
called Rat. He seemed to be in a good mood and said,
Yes, he could break away. Galatoire's? Sure. I should
go over, tell the maître d' I was meeting Captain Trapp.

—That's not going to do a damned bit of good, I
said.—You know they don't take reservations.

—That's right, he agreed.—You just do like I say,
son, and I'll see you there.

I was on my second beer when he breezed in and sat
down opposite me with a smile of mock surprise.

—My, Rat said.—I thought you'd still be outside. I
just wanted you over here to hold a place in line.

—Bullshit, I said.—I told the bastard I was meeting
you. He said you'd called, and pulled me in past a dozen
people.

His smile got broader, but he let it go. He had an
army sense of politics, fine and fully developed. He set
an envelope on the table between us.

—The short version is, Lester's gun fired *all* the shots.
No question about it. The silencer made a unique pattern. It was handmade.

—Not by that turkey. He couldn't even make his
wife.

—Some can, some can't. Anyhow, the DA's office loves it. I'm looklng more like a major all the time. I mean, hotdogging like this, and the Equal Employment Opportunity Commission . . .

—You ought to be ashamed.

—I am. If they offer me a gold leaf, I'm gonna turn it down.

His white wine and another beer came while we were laughing.

—Wes, I do appreciate you and Jesus keeping me plugged in. I don't want youall fooling around like that again, but I owe you one and a half.

Rat explained that Lester had taken leave of us by way of a massive heroin overdose. It seemed strange, since Lester had likely been born doing one organic chemical or another, but it happens. There was something stranger.

—That stuff was pure. I mean, they run it out at eighty-seven-percent pure dope. You can't hardly refine it better than that.

I realized then why Jesus had looked so surprised when he'd dipped into the glassine bag on Lester's table.

—How the hell do you account for that? I asked Rat.

—Well, he said, a little testily,—stuff happens.

—Maybe the guys in the laboratory were *doing* drugs while they were *making* drugs.

—Ha. So when they went for the powdered milk, they come up with more junk instead. That's good. I got to put that down.

—Does it bother you? I asked him.

—No, Rat said too quickly.—On account of I refuse to *be* bothered. It bothers you, though, don't it?

I looked at the menu and ordered what I always order at Galatoire's. Oysters en brochette, pompano amandine. No one deserves food that good. Even after you've paid the check, you feel like you stole it.

—Well, how did Lester get back on the street? I asked.

—Aha. Now *that* bothers me. Down at Charity, they want to blame it on Alphonse Delattre.

—Who the hell is . . .

—Detox clerk/orderly. She shuffled the admissions-and-release paperwork. They tell me they thought they'd let somebody named Mauvais Malancon out, but it was Lester. All Delattre's fault. Right papers, wrong ID.

—What does Alphonse have to say?

—Not squat. Alphonse has took off to Torrance, California. To advance himself. Left shortly after he made his error. Without telling anyone he'd made it—or telling anyone he was leaving. One of my people found out from an old girlfriend of his. *That* troubles me. Almost makes me want to go out to L.A. and speak to Alphonse while he's in the midst of advancing himself.

We ordered and sat silent. I was thinking of my own loose end. That phone call, invitation to a mass execution.

—Bullshit, Rat said.—You try to wrap up every little bitty thing, you'd get your pension before you cleared your first case. Let Lester sleep. Let Alphonse advance. Peace to all those poor folks who went off out of their time. I got me a rape-murder at the Argos Apartments that's gonna keep me on the street for a week. After he give her his Big Mac, he strangled the poor little old girl with her own panty hose. You fucking *know* that's wrong.

We ate and Rat allowed the food was pushing Sally's, but it cost too damned much. After all, it wasn't any *better* than Sally's. When I brought up the phone call, he gave me that sleepy-lidded special of his.

—You stlll want that list of folks who died at Bethel? Maybe you could run it down. Maybe somebody had an invention he wanted to show you. Maybe he had a surefire system for the track. Bag-a-Nag.

—You think I'd be wasting my time, don't you?

—Listen, I wasn't gonna tell you this. I mean like I don't want you to lose your self-esteem . . .

—What?

—I talked to the relatives of every one of those folks, see?

—Okay.

—And in the course of things, I brought up your

name, the paper, and all that. None of 'em ever heard of
you. Never heard their dead folks mention your name.

—You've gone too far. Denise knows me.

—Oh yeah. Hey, is it *Denise*? Well, yes, Denise Lemoyne knows you. I mean, she told me you'd come by
the house about doing an article on the old man. Said
her papa had been mean. Said he wouldn't give you the
waste water from out the commode. Mentioned she
wanted to look you up. I give her your address. Did I do
wrong?

—God bless you, Captain.

—To protect and to serve.

—You don't happen to sell aphrodisiacs, too, do you?

—Son, if you don't carry a bag of that stuff just below
your belt, you're shit out of luck.

We split then, and I went back to the paper, emptied
the envelope Rat had given me, and did a nice detailed
piece on Lester Grubbs, his putative motive, his weapon,
and his act. I wanted to use adjectives. I wanted to tell
the town how lucky they were that at least one piece of
filth had been flushed off the city streets. But no. I had
to go the other way and rub out every sign of Jesus and
me, of having any special knowledge of what had happened. Someone reading the story would have been
amazed to see Lester on the coroner's slab with that
neat third eye in the middle of his forehead, and no back
to his head at all. Personally, I hardly believe anything I
read.

Bob Pleasance was, by his standards, cordial.

—Now and then you make me remember why I pay
you, he told me.

—The reason you pay me is, I'm your bastard son by
the cleaning woman.

—Naw. You're not smart enough, and you drink like
a fish. Good job.

—Shit, I said,—I can do you a good job every day—if
I keep ending up in the middle of the story.

—What's wrong with that? Do it again, and I'll bump
you fifty a week. We got national coverage on this thing.

Your wrap-up is gonna get edited into the six o'clock news tonight. You want to bet?

—They'll never get Lester right. He had a certain piquancy.

—Yeah. The sonofabitch. One thing, though . . .

—Huh?

—I had Lucy Vaccaro go by the morgue. The girl's going ghoul on me. She said Lester Grubbs had a bullet hole the size of a golf ball smack through the middle of his head. You don't mention it, and there's nothing in the coroner's report.

—Maybe nobody noticed, I told him.

—What the fuck . . .

—It was an old wound. Lester got it in high school up home. Nothing serious. Shreveport boys don't cry.

When the phone rang, I was hoping it might be Denise Lemoyne. Nice idea. It was Jesus.

—You kind of dropped out of sight, I said.

—I been working.

—Not at the shop.

—I know this guy at Charity.

—About Grubbs? Rat filled me in.

—No, he didn't.

—Yeah, he did.

—You betting your *cojones*?

—Where are you?

—Nick's Hellenic.

—See you.

Nick's Hellenic Bar is one of those dumps that cater to sailors trying to waste their money while their ships are loaded or off-loaded down in the port. The food is greasy and plentiful and good and cheap. The drinks are okay, so long as you like ouzo and retsina and cheap American beer. The first two are fine with me. Jesus and I compromise on the second. He had a bottle open and working when I got there. The sun was melting the pavement outside, and retsina, chill as spring water, was all right. I ordered another bottle as soon as I sat down.

—Charity's got no record Grubbs was admitted, Jesus told me.—All that bullshit they gave Trapp was noise.

You look at their files, Grubbs wasn't never in that ward.

—Your friend ran a check?

—Every which way but *afuera*. No Grubbs. All that crap about Alphonse *fulano* just noise.

—What are you talking about? Did they make up Alphonse?

—Naw. He quit and went out west. Some hospital in Torrance. They just put it all on him. Like he did it himself.

—How do you know he didn't do it?

—I don't know he didn't do it. I just know he didn't do it by accident. My friend says you got to do six or seven things to clean an admission out of the files.

—Who did all this making-up stuff?

—What do I know? I guess they thought Rat was gonna drop it. Anyhow, nobody knows *how* Grubbs got lost. All they know, it wasn't no mistake.

—Even if they were right, Rat's happy just the way it is.

Jesus stared at me and sipped his wine. I chugged mine.

—I'm not, he said.

—You're not happy.

—Naw, man. I think this whole thing is bullshit.

—You're just pissed 'cause Lester OD'd before you holed him. *Machismo interrupto* . . .

Jesus laughed grudgingly.—Naw. It's wrong. That call you got . . . that hundred-proof dope. All this silly shit down at the hospital.

—You think Charity Hospital can't screw up its records?

—Sure. But how about the cops' records?

I hadn't thought of that. There had to be an arrest record from when the cops had picked Lester up at the Bethel and carted him over to Charity. The hospital end had vanished. But what about records at Central Lockup?

—Forget it, Jesus said.—They cleaned Lester's jacket, too. I got a friend over there. The last entry on Lester is that bank mess he was in.

I nodded. Jesus' friend was probably Frank Delery. I knew him too. A nice middle-aged man who lived alone and had no vices except that he did love to snort coke and carry on with his landlady. The police records were, as you might say, porous to anybody who could toke Frank now and again.

—It's wrong, Jesus said again.—I don't know what's going down, but it's something funny. Too many threads. If this thing was a drug deal, I wouldn't show for the buy.

I knew how he felt, but I didn't know if it meant anything. The longer you're on the streets, the tighter you get because you realize that there are circles within circles, incredibly complex situations in which people get killed almost as an afterthought. How bad can it get? I'll tell you how bad. I was wondering just then whether Rat was playing straight with us. I tried that out on Jesus

—Aw, man . . . First you don't know nothing. Then you go getting paranoid. Rat got himself a solved case. I mean, it looks like a solved case, right? Nobody upstairs is gonna backtrack him and yell, "Hey, asshole, you not finished."

—What about the DA? His old man got diced.

—So what? That dingdong don't know what day it is if the cops don't tell him. Sucker wants to go to Baton Rouge.

I didn't say anything. It made sense. Drew Lemoyne was politician enough to figure dead is dead. He'd want to milk the thing for sympathy, then get on with his undeclared campaign for governor. It looked as if they were going to put the whole mess away, leaving all those threads hanging. Jesus had a different idea.

—Look, he said.—You got any money?

—I can pay the rent.

—Can you make me a bail?

—What are you going to do?

—I'm gonna OD.

—What?

—They gonna find me somewhere stoned shitless. Real bad shape.

—You're *planning* it?

Jesus smiled.—Yeah. I think I need a few days in detox over at Charity.

I think the reason we did so well together was that Jesus moved faster than I did. But I could always pull him back when he was headed for the edge. Almost always.

—You think that's safe?

—Why not? If it's a paper fuck-up, I'll find out. If it's something else . . .

—That's what I mean. If it's something else.

—Hey, man, did your momma hand you an insurance policy when you got born?

—No. She didn't give me leftover brains, either.

—Look, it'll happen later, see? If I can do it right, you won't even need the bail money.

—What do you want me to do?

—Keep your ears open, baby. And your ass covered.

He left then. The heat was still something, and I wasn't in a hurry to hit the street, but I reached the bottom of the retsina and knew by the feeling in my stomach I wasn't ready for another one by myself.

When I walked outside, the clouds had gathered in convention over the city. As it began to rain, a few drops at first, then in cascades, torrents, I was on Iberville, walking toward a garage just off Bourbon where I'd left my car. I ducked into an oyster house, ordered a dozen on the half shell, and watched the sky darken to twilight in the middle of the day. Across the street, the buildings faded and almost vanished in the mist that rose from the street.

I thought about what Jesus was going to do. I didn't like it. Jesus was diving into the cesspool at Charity to find out if his brother had died an innocent bystander to a domestic quarrel that got out of hand—or whether there was something more, something deeper. If he found that something more, it wasn't going to be over. Not until some other people lost everything.

I thought he was all wet. Sure, there were threads hanging off Lester's visit to the Bethel. But the thing looked good enough to make a match and let it go. The paperwork screwup, my phone call . . . what the hell? I'd given up on the Colombians when I stepped into Lester Grubbs's room and found that MAC–10 in his lap. The greasers wouldn't have bothered planting it, doing all the setup. Why waste time trying to be clever? It's not cost-effective. Just murder everybody and walk away. No, Lester had done it, and Jesus was going in to find out nothing at all.

The rain slacked off enough for me to start walking again. I almost decided to go back to the paper, but Pleasance had Vaccaro to handle the crap, and I had a feature to finish. He'd want it for tomorrow. So that settled where I had to go next. I had to go where I wanted to go. Whether the DA wanted me around or not.

I stopped by my place and changed into dry clothes. I gathered up the scrapbooks Denise had left with me, a couple of legal pads, and some fine-line ballpoints. I was on my way out when I remembered I hadn't checked my answering machine. Forget it. Pleasance howling for the feature. So he could run it past Drew Lemoyne and all the other Uptown types mentioned or implied in it before he set it in type.

Aside from his half-assed editing, that seemed to be his chief function at the paper: making sure no one of substance was ruffled, given the least reason to mention to Holman at the next cocktail party that so-and-so had been troubled by such and such a reference in the paper. I smiled to myself. Pleasance was going to have his hands full with this one. He'd have to check back fifty years to find out if somebody's grandfather turned up in less than a favorable light.

The sun was out again when I parked in front of the house on State Street. I should have called. You don't just pop up and ring the doorbell at the nicer homes Uptown. Anyhow, Daddy might have changed his mind again and decided the feature was a very bad idea. The past hangs over New Orleans like those storm clouds that still moved slowly above. But no one digs it up.

One has one's money, one's home, one's position. No
need to unearth the rest. Someone once said that all
large fortunes are founded on great crimes. If there's
anything to that, logic suggests that moderate fortunes
are founded on a string of ordinary crimes. I hadn't
spotted a hint of that in Auguste's scrapbooks, but then
I wouldn't expect to.

Carole, the neat attractive maid, showed me in with
something like a smile. Under different circumstances, I
thought I might hustle her. Splendid legs, a tiny waist,
complexion the color of fine milk chocolate. But I returned her smile and took my accustomed place in the
library.

The garden was just as I had left it. Something like a
George Rodrigue painting, trunks of tall old trees dark,
wet and shining, leaves dripping from the rain just past.
The flowers and the grass seemed to have brightened,
become more intense since my last visit. I realized with
surprise how much I liked this room, this place, with its
illusion of permanence, its solidity, the finely wrought
sense that the Lemoynes had been here as long as there
had been anything at all. Even inside such a place, I was
the outsider, nose pressed against the glass, wishing I
knew how to get in to stay.

—Hello, she said from behind me, wrecking the fan-
tasy I was brewing—that I might see her in her string
bikini striding into the garden from the distant courtyard
behind, motioning me to come out and join her there.

—I saw you at the cathedral today. It was thoughtful
of you to come.

—I feel as though I knew him, I said.—Talking to
you, the scrapbooks . . .

—The Bethel Bar, she finished, her eyes darkening.

—You want to remember him sitting on his marble
bench in the garden, I told her.—The way it ended for
him was an accident. It didn't mean anything.

She nodded gratefully and motioned me to a seat at
the library table. I realized that she was still wearing the
black dress I'd seen her in earlier. It took nothing from
her looks. Beautiful women mourn beautifully.

I pointed to the scrapbooks I'd set down in another chair and put my pad on the mahogany table.—I have a lot of questions, I said.

—All right. But first, there's something I want you to hear.

Denise walked across to a small stereo system set under the windows that looked out on the garden. She put a cassette into the player and pressed a couple of buttons. Then she stood with her back to me, as if there were someone in the garden she was watching.

". . . it was the summerof 1935 then, and he'd managed to turn the state into an armed camp. His own people were armed to the teeth, and of course he had the state police and the National Guard if he needed that. On the other side there was the Square Deal Association, and dozens of small local groups that preached patriotism and . . ."

If Denise had been looking at me when the tape began to play, she would have thought I was having a seizure. The chill ran down my spine and into my gut, lying there like cold steel. No doubt, no question. The voice I was hearing on the tape was the voice I had heard on the phone, the voice that had summoned me to the Bethel Bar.

CHAPTER
8

HOLY CHRIST, I BLURTED OUT.—THAT'S HIM.
—My grandfather, Denise murmured, still looking out into the garden.

—No, I mean—okay, your grandfather. But that's the voice I heard on the phone . . . the man who told me to meet him at the Bethel Bar.

She turned back to face me then, a look of surprise on her face.

—That's . . . It doesn't seem likely, does it?

—No. But it's true.

—Why would Grand-père want to meet someone he didn't know at the Bethel Bar?

—Denise, listen. It's him. It's not a probable. It's a certain. Shit, I've heard him in my dreams since. . . .

—Wes, I don't doubt you. But voices . . . a lot of older people sound alike.

The load of pig iron was still in my belly. I wished I were somewhere else. Too much was churning in my

head for me to be charming. I needed to figure where all
this could possibly go, and when I start thinking, I get
irritable. I can't help it. Thinking is hard.

—Tell me exactly what he said to you. Can you remember? she asked in something close to a patronizing
tone.

—Yeah, I came back at her.—I remember. Like I
remember slipping and almost falling on the blood when
I . . .

My voice stopped as if I'd torn out my own throat.
That wasn't something I'd meant to say to her. But she
let it go by.

—Tell me . . .

—He said for me to meet him at the Bethel Bar. He
said he had a story for me. He'd tell me about the . . .
deduction box. Then he hung up.

I barely got the last sentence out. Denise looked the
way I must have when I first heard her grandfather's
voice on that tape. Her face went white, and I thought
she was going to pass out.

—Why don't you get us a drink? she said at last.
—There's brandy in the secretary.

I went over, opened the front of the secretary, and
found a decanter and some snifters. I poured a couple of
heavy slugs, keeping my eyes on Denise all the time. I
couldn't read her. Was it just an increment of the sadness she already felt? Or something more? Something
like a horror? I carried the brandy over to the library
table and slapped back half of mine as I sat down.

—You're sure about what he said?
—Yes.

—Did you . . . did you know what he was talking
about?

—You mean the deduction box? No.

—You never heard of it? The deduct box?

I stared at her. Obviously she had.—No, I never did.
What is it?

She swallowed hard, then started speaking in a low,
almost mechanical voice, as if she were quoting her own
senior thesis.

—The deduct box belonged to Huey Long. It was where he kept his campaign cash. No, not really. It was more than that. It was his slush fund. They called it the deduct box because every state employee had to kick back part of his salary to keep it full.

—Sounds like a great way to stay solvent—and illegal as hell.

She laughed a little grimly.—Huey wasn't a stickler for legality. He was too good a lawyer.

I shrugged.—Okay, so Huey stole, and what he stole he kept in the . . . deduct box. But what would your grandfather know about it? And why would he think it was worth a story fifty years later?

—When Huey Long was assassinated, Denise went on in that same low voice,—the deduct box disappeared. They tried to find it for years.

—It never turned up?

—Never. Not a sign, not a trace.

—Okay. You can put it next to the safe in the *Andrea Doria*. It's worth a paragraph in somebody's brief history of Louisiana.

—People say it was worth a good deal more than that. They say there was at least a million dollars in it . . . and something more.

—A million?

—And papers guaranteed to ruin most of Huey's enemies. Affidavits, transcripts, legal documents he'd picked up one way or another, private papers. No one knew just what was in the box, or who it might incriminate.

—Okay . . . one more time. Auguste Lemoyne was a diehard anti-Long man. How would he know anything about it?

She looked away, but I could read her mind. No need to press, to say aloud what we were both thinking.

—Let's try it another way. Why would he want to tell *me* what he knew? We'd never laid eyes on one another.

—He knew of you. He read your series on capital punishment. One evening at supper, he read us the section where you recommended publishing pictures of the victims—just so people would know exactly why some of those animals at Angola were being executed. He said you sounded like Oliver Cromwell.

Coming from a French south Louisiana Catholic, that didn't figure to be a compliment.—He thought I was wrong?

—No. He said in his old age all the softness had left him. He told me . . . he hadn't realized in his youth how hard, how cruel, the human heart can be. Cold-blooded crimes should be punished. Coldly. Otherwise, none of us could live decently.

So much for the "why me" question. It seemed Auguste Lemoyne and I had held similar views. He might have enjoyed a drink with Rat Trapp and Jesus and me. Or maybe not. He could have found us too lenient, too much given to looking the other way on the softer sins.

The two of us sat for a few minutes watching the sun's rays breaking through the clouds, transfiguring the garden. I reckoned the next step was for me to listen to all the tapes her grandfather had made for her, which she told me were the basis of her senior thesis: the living words of someone who'd taken part in the battles of the thirties. Maybe I'd find something there. At least now I had reason to wonder what there might be to find. And yet . . .

What was there that could bear on the killings at the Bethel? Likely nothing. It seemed Auguste Lemoyne had simply picked the wrong bar at the worst possible time. And if I hadn't been waylaid by Jesus, I'd have made the same mistake.

—A million is a lot of money, I mused.

—I've heard so, Denise replied coolly.

—How do you reckon your grandfather could have known anything about it?

That look again.—I really couldn't say. He never mentioned it in the tapes. He met Huey Long just once. At a trial or a hearing of some kind. Huey told him he was a very clever lawyer. He told Grand-père when he grew sick of working for the dead and the dying, he could have a job with the state.

—The dead . . .?

Denise laughed ironically.—That's what Senator Long called us—our kind of people. The ones who founded this city, kept it going for . . . centuries.

—Surrendered it to the Yankees in 1862. Without firing a shot.

Her smile was withering.—Why, yes. That was clever, don't you think? We did a little better than Charleston or Atlanta or Richmond.

She was right. The other towns had died fighting, and been burned to the ground. New Orleans survived. We stared at each other coldly. We'd just touched the Difference, the wedge between us. It had nothing to do with money or class. It had to do with the way we looked at life, with what you saved and what you threw away, what was worth keeping at any price—and what finally didn't matter at all.

—Is there anything else? she asked me after a moment, her voice as remote as a long-distance operator's.

—I don't know, I said.—Is there?

She melted then.—I'd like to help you with the article about Grand-père. I'd like to do him that last service.

So there was that. A feature story praising, recalling the dead. I considered as how Huey had probably been right.

—I think we have to clear up this phone call.

She looked almost frightened then.—You really think it's important?

—I really do. Your grandfather was there to meet me.

—You don't think that had anything to do with . . .

—I don't know. If I had to bet a lot of money, I'd say no. But I want to check it out. It's a hell of a way to end the story anyway, isn't it?

Denise nodded silently.—There's one possibility, she said.—We could go talk to Father John.

—The priest at St. Louis Cathedral?

She nodded.—He was Grand-père's oldest friend. They went to high school together. He was Grand-père's confessor.

—Then he won't be having much to say, will he?

—Nothing he heard in the confessional.

—Or out. If it might be embarrassing.

That angered her.—You think we have something to hide, she snapped at me.

—Baby, I really don't know. The old man had a story to tell. Something about the deduct box. Then all the talking stopped.

—Come on, she said sharply.—We'll take my car.

It was a quick silent ride down St. Charles Avenue and into the Quarter in her Mercedes 280 convertible. Denise's hair blew out behind, and I had a chance to look at her without her looking back. She had a beautiful profile, a long straight nose that tilted at the tip just the least bit. She was still wearing that tight black dress and her breasts pressed against it when she breathed deeply. Her expression was chill and determined, and she acted as if she were driving alone. That was all right. I looked at her legs, thighs pressing against the thin fabric of her dress as it hitched up above her knees. They were not the legs of a girl, round and soft and full. They were a woman's legs with some of the softness gone, the least bit of muscle showing, something taut and fine in them.

I was wishing I'd kept my damned mouth shut about New Orleans and its rich when we parked near the cathedral. There is no cure for history, no way to set it right. A few serious fires in a hundred libraries and history itself would begin to turn back into myth, each generation's memories of what had passed before becoming thinner, less precise. The past was nothing for a man and woman to argue about. The past wasn't much of anything. In fact, it was nothing at all.

Denise turned to me, reached over and took my hand, stopping me as I was about to get out of the car.

—Sorry, we both said, almost in unison.

—I kept hearing myself the whole way down here, she said.—I sounded like a rich Uptown bitch.

—I sounded like a sullen redneck, I said.

We grinned together.

—It doesn't make sense to argue about the dead.

—Or the dying, she answered, a little somberly.

—What do you say we argue about each other? I suggested.—There'll be plenty of reasons.

Denise smiled, nodded. I squeezed her hand and we headed for the rectory.

An elderly black woman who recognized Denise offered her condolences on Mister Auguste, and told us Father Cunningham was in the cathedral.

We stopped in the garden for a moment. Denise reached for my hand again.

—Sometimes after Mass, we'd stop out here, she said softly. —We'd have our own prayer and sit still awhile, then go back to the car and drive out to Delmonico's for Sunday dinner.

It was a strange place, quiet, shadowed. As we stood there it was as if we were alone in the deep silence of a monastery. Yet only yards away was the bustle and murmur of Royal Street.

—You're not going to let your grandfather go away, are you?

—Not ever, Denise said, a thread of steel in her voice.

—He was my first great love. I guess I'll always measure other men by him.

We walked to the side door of the cathedral and stepped inside as I wondered how I'd measure up to the old man. I decided that was a hopeless question. On one hand, Auguste Lemoyne and I had nothing in common at all. But on the other, I gave up trying to follow the workings of a woman's mind a long time ago. If they don't care about you, nothing fits. If they love you, everything falls into place.

Inside the church, it was dark. Only candles before statues here and there, the sanctuary light, and a few lights behind the altar illuminated the place. My first impression was, Why don't they keep this place clean? It seemed there was paper and rubbish all over the floor. An instant later, I realized that was absurd. St. Louis Cathedral never has paper and rubbish on the floor. My eyes accustomed themselves to the shadows, and I saw that the rubbish was chunks of plaster scattered in front of the foremost rank of pews.

—Wes, Denise started to say. Then she pointed up and over to the side altar on our left.

It was in shambles, as if someone had taken a sledge-hammer and pick to it. The tabernacle had been broken open, the marble of the altar itself ripped loose and thrown down to break in pieces on the floor. I stepped behind the altar rail to get a closer look and almost fell down as I tripped over the wreckage of a statue lying there.

Someone had done a number on Christ. They had knocked off his arms, his head, and had used a crowbar or a screwdriver on his body. Out of the darkness, I could see his painted eyes staring up at me, pained but with infinite patience. I had less. My experience told me anyone who'd do it to a statue would likely do it to a human being. A moment later, it turned out I was right.

—Oh, my God . . . Wes . . .

I couldn't see her, but I vaulted across the altar rail in the direction of her voice and almost ran over her in the shadows. She was kneeling in the center aisle beside something. For a moment, I thought it was another statue, another piece of mindless destruction. I was half-right.

I knelt down beside Denise, who was holding Father Cunningham's head. It was too dark to tell much, but blood was running down his face into her lap. He seemed to be bleeding from the nose and ears. His eyes were open, staring, squinting as if the light was too bright. Maybe it was. For him.

—Forgiveness . . . time won't heal it. Boys, boys, in the name of God, how could you? No, no, don't say that. You know better. There's always time for . . .

—What's he trying to say? I asked Denise. But she was crying and could only shake her head. I pulled her loose from him and put my folded jacket under his head.

—Go back to the rectory, I told her.—Tell the old lady what's happened. Call the police and tell them to get an ambulance here as fast as they can. Ask them to get hold of Captain Ralph Trapp in homicide. Say they should mention my name. Can you remember all that?

She nodded like a mechanical doll, her eyes on the old priest. I had to push her toward the door. Even then, she paused in the distant shadows as if she had no power to go on.

—Goddamnit, I called after her,—you're gonna lose him if you don't get us some help.

She ran out then, and I turned back to the old man. I went up to the main altar and grabbed a pair of candles, a poor ignorant Protestant raiding the Lord's table to light his servant's grievous hour. Then I tried to see if Father Cunningham had been shot or stabbed, listening all the time to his reverie.

—Under the seal of the Sacred Heart, you hear? All that money that no one can use, secrets no one can ever know . . . Ah, lads, you'd never trust one another. God help you, you'd not even trust me. . . . It's a door that has to stay closed . . . forever.

I couldn't find any wounds—except what they'd done to his head. One of his temples seemed to move freely as he breathed. It had to be a fractured skull. Why he was still alive, I couldn't say. How he was talking, even babbling, was more than I could figure out. Then, suddenly, the old man grabbed the front of my shirt, trying to pull himself up. It seemed that his eyes were focused on me, burning through me as if he could see the dark outback and secret steppes of my soul.

—If it weren't for your families, he snarled at me in bitterness and anger.—So help me God, if it weren't for your families, I'd hand you over . . .

—Father, try to lie still, I told him.—You're going to be all right, I lied.

It was a lie, because when he started up, my hand had reached behind his head to keep him from falling, hurting himself even worse. When he eased back against my hand, I could feel that his skull behind was pulp filled with needles and slivers of bone. I'm not going to throw up, I told myself. I can do that later. Oh, God, I wish I was a priest, some kind of Catholic, so I could give him absolution or last rites or whatever it is they do.

His eyes hadn't left me. I had his full strained attention.—Do you know what you've done to me? he asked hoarsely, both bloody hands caught in my shirt.—Do you know that this could be the damnation of me?

—Not a chance, I said like a fool, wanting to enter into whatever kind of hallucination he was having, make it easier for him.—You did right. Whatever you did, it was all right.

— . . . the sin of it, the awful sin of it, bound under the Sacred Heart. . . .

—Right, I said.—The Sacred Heart . . .

Then there was a change in his expression. The anger and fear faded, and his eyes grew cold, demanding. The reediness in his voice changed to strength. He surged upward, full of strength and merciless anger.

— . . . damn you for murderers every one. You'll come here and do penance, do you hear? Do you hear me, damn you . . . ? There'll be no end to it . . . Ash Wednesday . . .

He had hold of my shirt, almost pulling me down on top of him, his eyes burning up at me out of the darkness as if he knew it all, every evil I had done or wanted to do, every time I had missed the mark. Then, as suddenly as it had come, the strength drained from him and he was a rag doll in my arms. I thought for a moment he was gone, but there was still a pulse at his throat and shallow breathing. I held him as best I could, as if so holding him would send my energy, my strength into him. Then the lights throughout the cathedral began flickering on, and I could see in the soft glow of the chandeliers hanging above that the old priest was hurt even worse than I had thought.

One of his eyes was ruined, the skull crushed in above it, the cheekbone broken below. His right ear was almost severed from his head. I wanted to be sick the way I had needed to be in the Bethel Bar, but it wasn't going to happen. Puking is a luxury when people need you. Then I knew Denise was back beside me because I heard her gasp and choke, and then cry out, her voice mounting, wailing like that of an old woman mourning her last son.

—Knock off the shit, I told her roughly. Not for his sake or even mine. For hers.—If you want to put on a performance, there'll be plenty of time.

I still couldn't see her because I didn't want to put Father Cunningham's head down again. My arm was under his shoulders, and I thought, if I held him that way, there might be no more damage to his brain in back where he had no solid skull left at all. As if it mattered.

We waited for what seemed an autumn and deep into winter until the ambulance team got there, and I let an intern take my place. My shirt was soaked with the priest's blood, and I found I couldn't walk very well. Denise was kneeling on the cold marble floor near the altar rail, her forehead resting against it. I went to her and helped her up.

—He's dead, she said woodenly.

—No, I told her.—He's not dead. It's very bad, but he's not dead.

—He's . . . dying.

—That could be.

—Like Huey Long told my grandfather . . . the dead . . . and the dying.

—Put that out of mind, I told her, drawing her close to me, ignoring the blood on my sleeve and down the front of my shirt.—Huey said a lot of things. His mouth wasn't a prayer book.

Denise looked up at me, and even behind her tears, the beauty was there.

—God, you're so . . . north Louisiana.

—I can do East Texas in different voices if you like that better.

—Oh, Wes, she sobbed, and I took her to one of the pews and sat with her as the intern and ambulance people worked at getting an IV into Father Cunningham, then lifted him onto a gurney and moved out the side door just as the police began to arrive. Rat was in the second wave and called off some snot-nosed uniformed punk with a pencil mustache and a clipboard who wanted to know all about it. Rat looked tired and somber and acknowledged Denise with a nod. Then he detached me from her and took me over to one side.

—Man, nothing happens anymore but you're right there.

—It comes for me, baby. What can I do?

—For a start, how about you leave Denise Lemoyne at home?

—You don't want to get into that, sweetness. Do I ever hassle you about your women?

—You don't *know* none of my women. Anyhow, listen to what I'm saying. I don't need Drew Lemoyne staring down my throat on account of my friends diddling his daughter.

—Tell the EEOC, good buddy, I grinned.—You gonna ask me about the old priest?

—Youall come in the church, there he was.

—Okay, I see I'm going to have to take over. Why were we here?

—Priest was an old friend of the family. Baptized the girl, married the girl's father and mother, buried the grandfather. Courtesy call. Maybe you want to start taking instructions to be a Catholic, 'cause Denise won't . . .

—We came to talk to him. Denise played some tapes her grandfather had made to help her work on Louisiana history.

Rat looked at me as if I had lost an oar.—Louisiana history . . . Man, what are you going on about?

—The voice on the tapes was the voice that called me. His expression changed.—What?

—It was August Lemoyne who called me at the paper, told me to meet him at the Bethel.

Rat pursed his lips and looked up toward the ceiling of the cathedral.—You wouldn't be saying that if you wasn't sure.

—No.

He sighed then, as if I'd placed some awful weight on him. Or maybe replaced one already there.—Well, shit, Rat said.—I'm gonna have to think about that.

—That's what I was doing.

—So you come to see the old priest. Just in case he

might know how come Auguste called you. What else? You talk to him?

—You see what I saw. Some crazy sonofabitch came in and went to breaking up Christ. I guess Father Cunningham came in and complained.

—Ummm. Tore that altar over there on the side all to pieces. Busted up the altar stone. Did that to the Sacred Heart . . .

My head must have snapped around. I looked at Rat, then over at the altar.—The Sacred Heart . . .

—What about the Sacred Heart? Rat asked me.

—Nothing. I'm a Methodist. We take the Lord in one piece.

—You so cute. Old man say anything when you found him?

—Nothing you could make sense of, I lied. I had to think about what Father Cunningham had been babbling, to judge whether it meant anything or not. Rat didn't want Drew Lemoyne on his back while he was working. I didn't want Rat on mine. I'd told him about Auguste Lemoyne being the one who'd called me. What else was I supposed to tell him? He already knew that Huey Long was dead.

The place was filling with people by then. The old black woman stood beside another aged priest. I think they were both weeping. The punk with the mustache was strutting around as if he'd just bought the real estate under the church, asking people questions that didn't mean anything, demanding answers that nobody could give. He reminded me of Lester Grubbs somehow. Rat was watching him, too.

—Sonofabitch is a probationary patrolman. Bucking for chief.

—I wish you'd bust his ass.

—I think I will.

—Listen, I've got to take care of Denise. She's going to want to go to the hospital. The old man baptized her.

—I'll send her in a squad car.

—You going to keep me here?

—No. But I got this bad feeling about you.

—What . . . ?

—I don't know what you know, but you know. Something to do with old man Lemoyne calling you. Whatever it is, you're keeping it to yourself.

—Come on, Rat . . .

—Don't shit me, man. I can read you like a road sign.

—If I had anything, I'd tell you.

—How about if you had something that didn't amount to anything?

—I'd wait till I could make sense out of it. Then I'd tell you.

Rat looked at me for a long moment, then nodded.
—You get back to me, hear?

I walked over to the pew where Denise was sitting alone. She was shivering in the moist heat.

—Come on. They took him to Charity. Rat's going to send us over in a police car.

She rose and took my arm, and we walked back toward the side entrance. My foot hit something, and I leaned down to pick it up. For a moment, my brain couldn't register what my eyes saw. Then I realized that it was the plaster Sacred Heart itself, torn from the breast of the broken statue, isolated, wound with a circlet of thorns, a small flame glowing at its top.

—Oh, God, Denise sobbed, and turned away.

I walked up to the ruined altar and placed the piece of scarlet plaster on the base where the statue had stood. Then I guided Denise past a knot of staring shocked people, through the door, and out into the night.

CHAPTER
9

WE WERE AS SILENT ON THE WAY TO THE HOSPITAL AS we'd been driving downtown a few hours before. Not because we were angry with one another, but because we were drained. I looked as if I'd stepped in front of a trolley, my shirt drenched in blood. Denise's skirt was dark with it, and when we reached Charity and went in through the emergency room door, an orderly or two looked at us anxiously as if we were walking wounded.

They were working on Father Cunningham in one of the cubicles across from where we stood. Now and then we could hear raised voices from the doctors behind the curtain. They weren't celebrating another milestone of medical progress.

I tried to get her to move out of the hallway, down to the waiting room, but it was no good.—He might call for me, she said. I didn't think so.

—When I was a little girl, Father John and Grand-père

took me everywhere. It was as if I belonged to both of
them. They knew I loved Pontchartrain Park, the Ferris
wheel, the merry-go-round. Sometimes, after Mass and
lunch at Delmonico's . . . Father John said there was no
better way to keep the Sabbath Day holy . . . than to
make a little girl happy.

—How about your father?

Denise looked away from me.—He . . . had a career
to build, family interests to see to. We weren't close.

—It's better now?

—Why would you think so?

—It was better with my father after I was grown.

—I'm glad. I suppose what passes between fathers
and sons is awfully important to both of them.

—I guess so.

—Did you love your father? she asked me.

—I'm not sure that's the word to use. I guess you
could say we . . . mostly lived up to one another's
expectations.

Denise smiled and held on to my hand.—That's quite
a lot, isn't it?

—I guess so. Nowadays.

—Wes . . . ?

—Yes.

—Do you always know what's right? Like Cromwell?

—I know what's right for me.

—Always?

—So far.

—That's astonishing.

—I don't always do what's right.

—Thank God.

We both laughed then, despite ourselves. Probably
because the tension had gone on too long. I wasn't sure
Denise knew what we were waiting for, but I did. That
wound the tension all the more tightly. The release felt
good, and I reached down and kissed her cheek. It was
cool and soft and fragrant all at once. I had never wanted
so much to make love to a woman. While we were
snuggling and giggling, we heard her father's voice behind us.

—Denise . . .

We turned together, arms still interlocked. Drew Lemoyne's expression probably wouldn't have been much different if he'd caught us sacked out in a crummy Quarter hotel. But, being a gentleman, he simply pummeled me a little with his eyebrows and addressed his words to Denise.

—How is he?

—I don't know. No one has told us anything.

Lemoyne grudgingly turned to me. I shrugged, not wanting to say more than Denise was prepared to hear.

—They hurt him bad, I said.—Fractured skull. Likely multiple fractures.

—I went by the cathedral. Captain Trapp doesn't seem to have much. Some gold candlesticks missing, a man seen running in Decatur Street.

—That's not much to have. A broken statue and a broken priest. Maybe somebody doesn't like religion.

—That's insane.

—It's crazy to go into a bar and machine-gun everybody, but it happens.

—But . . . Grubbs is dead. What does the bar incident have to do with . . .

I let my mouth get ahead of my brain. It's a problem with me, but this time it happened because I didn't like Lemoyne. I didn't like his snotty Uptown style, and I didn't like the way he'd looked at Denise and me—as if he'd rather see her buried in roaches than with my arm around her. Most of all, I didn't like his air of command and superiority. I suspected that, stripped of his inheritance and his political clout, he was just like most people. Fucked up and uncertain.

—I went to the Bethel Bar because your father called me. I think he had a story he wanted to tell. Denise and I went to the cathedral to talk to Father Cunningham. To see if he might know what your father wanted me to hear.

His face closed down like the metal awning on a

Middle Eastern shop. Denise's gasp pulled my eyes away from him.

—Wes, you think Grand-père and Father John were both . . .

—What can I tell you, baby? I go to talk to two old men. One's been killed when I get there. The other's battered half to . . .

Just then, one of the doctors exited the cubicle where they'd been working on the old priest. As he walked toward us I recognized Hugh D'Anton, the chief of staff. On ER duty? At night? Drew Lemoyne walked over to meet him. The two of them stood caught up in conversation, intense, almost argumentative. D'Anton was a tall, handsome man whose dark hair was going not gray but silver. I didn't know his ordinary expression, but the way he was looking at Lemoyne would pass for towering anger on any stage in the country. What the hell did he have to be mad at the DA for? Was he one of Cunningham's parishioners, wanting to know why Lemoyne hadn't dragged the perpetrator in along with the victim?

—It's as if somebody's trying to destroy my whole world, Denise whispered hoarsely.

—No, I told her.—That's just a side effect. There's something else going on.

The conversation broke off, and D'Anton stallked away down the hall as Drew Lemoyne, looking pale, shaken, came back to us. He reached out clumsily for Denise's hands. As if he didn't know how to be comforting, as if he'd never learned.

—He's gone, darling. Father John is gone.

Denise burst into tears and turned back to me, leaving her father's arms stretched out in space. I was too concerned about her to pay attention to him.

—Why would anyone want to kill him? Denise cried out.

—I don't know, I said.—But I'm going to.

We sat on one of the benches, and I tried to explain that this wasn't the end of anything. I'd be on the story till there wasn't any story left. So would Rat.

—You can't bring back the dead, but you can send them some company, I told her.

Denise stopped crying. She looked at me, her eyes no longer filled with tears, as if her anger had boiled them away.—I want that, she said in a low voice.—God forgive me, I want that. I want to see it happen.

—No, I said.—You want it, but you don't want to see it.

When I looked up, Lemoyne was staring at me. He wanted badly to say something, but decided this wasn't the time for it. He told Denise he'd take her home. They'd have to be preparing for another funeral.

—Will you drive my car out to the house? she asked me.

—Sure, I said.—I'll put the keys in your mailbox.

Denise said she'd call me in the morning, and I left ahead of them, caught a taxi, and went back to the *Item*.

When I walked into the city room, I could see Bob Pleasance through the glass panel back in his office on the phone. He caught my eye, and gave me one of those imperious gestures of his. Get the hell back here, it said. I should resist my lower impulses, but I never do. I popped him the Ancient Manual Salute and went to my desk. Somebody had been using my screen, so the computer was hot, and I opened a document and had the story half-finished before Pleasance was done with his phone call and came to the door of his office.

—Mr. Colvin, may I have a minute of your time?

—Certainly, Mr. Pleasance.

When I got back there, he was steaming. Somehow, when Pleasance was angry, it always made me want to laugh. I think he'd never been effective in his whole dumb life. His anger was as pointless as the rest of his personality.

—You give me the finger again in front of the staff, and I'll can you.

—Sweet. In a week or so, the bass will be tearing the low limbs off the trees over on the north shore.

—I'm serious.

—Bullshit. You might fire me, but you're never serious.

That was an average exchange. He wasn't going to fire me, and I wouldn't pop him the bird if he laid off the Big Boss routine.

—Trapp wants you to call him.

—Okay.

—He said . . . you were there again.

—Yeah. He was kinda hacked about it.

—You blame him? What would you think if somebody kept turning up everywhere people were dying?

—Why, I'd say he was one hell of a newspaperman, I drawled.

—You've got the story?

—Everything there is. Get Vaccaro to dig up Father Cunningham's clips. He's been at the cathedral a long time.

—Trapp said no leads?

—Nothing you could give the DA. Even if you were into giving stuff to the DA.

—Speaking of the DA, you were with his daughter.

Rat hadn't told him I was with Denise. It wasn't his style. I wondered who had.

—Remember that feature on Auguste Lemoyne? Denise and I were trying to get some background from Father Cunningham. I guess we should have been quicker.

—You see any connection between the killings?

—What an idea. Someone is killing the grand old men of New Orleans? It's not even a movie title.

He nodded, and I started to go back to work. Pleasance's voice stopped me at the door.—She's Holman's goddaughter, you know.

—What?

—Denise Lemoyne. A word to the wise . . .

—I'm not wise, and he's not a Catholic.

Some kind of dispensation. Holman thinks a lot of her. Why don't you stick with the doxies in the Quarter?

I could feel my face burning.—Why don't you give

your wife a break and fuck your fist, I answered, and walked out.

When I got back to my desk and calmed down, I finished my own version of murder in the cathedral and sent it in to Pleasance. On my way out. I never talk to him about a story. He once told me there were three grammatical errors in Keats's "Ode to a Nightingale." I just send in the stuff, and he does what he wants with it. I get a check every two weeks, and we mostly leave each other alone.

I walked out into the hot humid night and started down toward the cathedral. I'd never driven a Mercedes sports car, and I was looking forward to it. I wondered if I'd actually buy one—even if I had a lot of loose bucks.

As I walked up the street, I was thinking about another bottle of retsina at Nick's Hellenic, but it was too far away, and nobody drops into that neighborhood late without a crowbar or a pistol. I wasn't going to drive Denise's car over there and invite the local slime to carve me up and make off with the Mercedes. I was into Decatur Street when I saw the car parked up ahead. It looked as if it were making eighty just standing still. I was about a half block away when the headlights went on, and the car started toward me.

For a moment I thought Denise had decided to wait for me, had sent her father on home. I liked thinking that. If she needed me to help her make it through the night, it was going to be one hell of a night.

I stepped off the pavement to wave her down. As I did so, my mind was on Denise, on how it felt to hold her close even when death and dying were all around us.

Thinking of her that way almost killed me. Literally. Because I expected the car to slow down and pull up beside me. I expected to see her. But it wasn't slowing down, and at the last instant, I realized what was happening and spun around, falling back up onto the sidewalk as the car smashed against the curb inches from my head. I could see the tire compress, sparks and chips of concrete fly away as the wheel and axle shagged along the curb for six or eight feet. Then I was up on my knees, onto my feet, and running.

Whoever was behind the wheel wasn't a quitter. He gunned the engine, pulled away from the curb, and barreled along the street behind me again. There were no cars parked where I was running, and when I took a chance and looked back over my shoulder, I could see the Mercedes coming at me with two tires up on the sidewalk and accelerating.

I was breathing hard and trying to figure where and how to make a move, panic pushing me along at a pretty good speed. Scared shitless, I might be able to outrun a quarter horse for fifty yards. My mind was calmly noting what bad shape I was in, how the cigars and cigarettes and booze and shameful hours had broken me down, left me a panting, slavering victim of whoever was piloting that car. Less calmly, I was telling my brain to fuck off. Nobody can outrun a Mercedes.

If I cut into the street, I was dead. The far side was a solid block of blank warehouse wall. As I ran, I couldn't see far down my side, so I tried to remember. Christ, I walked this way five days a week. Then I realized I was coming up fast on a furniture store. Glass show windows, and a door inset maybe five or six feet back from the street. If the guy in Denise's car had a gun, that was no place to be. But if he was determined to do the job with the Mercedes, I might have a chance. What the hell, if he had a gun, why didn't he just stop and use it?

I saw the doorway coming up just as I realized my eyes were getting foggy, that I was on the way to passing out. The last thing I remember clearly is doing a hook slide into that doorway, through the door and the glass, like an NFL quarterback with fifteen hundred pounds of defensive linemen coming for him at just below the velocity of light.

I hit the floor inside on some kind of rug, and as I

rolled, it seemed the whole front of the store behind me
exploded. I went on crawling, scuttling like a crab, trying
to get under a conference table or anything that would
give me shelter. Then I realized I didn't hear the roar of
that engine any longer. For a moment, I didn't hear
anything at all. Then there was the distant sound of
footsteps, of someone running outside in the street.

There wasn't any hurry. Whatever the status was, it
was going to stay that way. I got my breathing back
down to a choked rasping fight for air, and tried to sit
up. Slowly. There was no light in the place until I got to
my knees, found a table lamp, and switched it on, staying
low in case my guess about the gun was wrong. I had a
long shallow cut on my left arm, and another one on my
chest. I sat there looking at the fresh blood flowing out
onto the dried blood on my shirt, and I remember thinking, There's a $22.50 shirt shot to hell.

After a few minutes, when I realized no one was
coming in for me, and that I wasn't dying on my own, I
got up and walked back to the front of the store. I'd
wrecked the door myself, but the Mercedes had managed the rest. The front of the car had gone all the way
through the show window, smashing up a nice dining
room set, and was resting on the back of an amazingly
ugly overstuffed sofa, one tire still spinning. There was
no one behind the wheel, but the seat was full of broken
glass, and a sliver of blue from a streetlight outside
seemed to be glancing off spots of blood on the dash-
board. Good, I thought. I hope the glass cut your fucking throat. Better still, save your throat. Lose your nuts.
And live a thousand years.

I was still shaking badly, and sat down in a tacky
chair that matched the sofa. Then I almost lost it when
the burglar alarm suddenly began to ring. I believe I
started laughing. Or hooting. I had just gotten myself
under control when the cops started arriving.

When the hassle was over with—or at least put on
hold—I was sitting in Rat's office with bandages here
and there. I had felt better in my time. I hoped to feel

better again. Just then, it wasn't going well. Rat was staring at me the way he looked at suspects.

—Okay, you didn't drive the fucking car through the goddamned store.

—No, I didn't.

—I'm gonna believe that.

—Thanks.

—You're sober.

—Not by choice.

He opened his desk drawer and drew out a fifth of Irish whiskey. The man has impeccable taste. Ten years in the army does wonders for a kid raised in the projects.

—I ought to be ashamed. Lost my hospitality. It's this job. I don't hardly ever give a jolt to a suspect.

—Lot of 'em get one later, don't they?

We smiled, and things got right between us again.

—No way it was an accident?

—No way, I said.—The first time, when he bounced off the curb, I could believe it. But he came after me again. I ran a block before I found that furniture store.

He nodded, but I knew he wasn't convinced.—You know whose car it is?

—Sure. That's why I stepped out there and let him get that first crack at me.

—Thought she was coming back for you?

—Yes.

—Why'd you think that?

I laughed out loud and took another belt of the Irish. —Christ, what's wrong with you? I thought it because I wanted it to be so. I wanted her to come back. I want her right now. When I wake up in the morning, I'm gonna be wanting her worse than I do now.

Rat shook his head.—I guess you got a better shot than some street nigger from Fisher project. But not a whole hell of a lot better.

That pissed me off, but there wasn't anything to say. He was probably right.

—How do you feel about me going home? I asked him.—My ass is in a sling. I need to sleep.

—Stick around. Have one more.

—What for? Are you still wondering if I tried to run myself down?

—Man, I never thought that. I saw the curb all chewed up. I saw where you went through that door. Anyhow, the car was hot-wired. You had keys, didn't you?

He paused then. He was going over it one more time.

—And?

—I still got to think it was some fucking kid who found him some hot wheels parked over by the cathedral. He couldn't pass 'em up, and he couldn't keep 'em. So how about tooling around for a while, then scaring the piss out of some of the locals. Beats another night dicking around at the Burger King.

It was just goofy enough to be true. It happened all the time. Uptown, downtown. Cars vanished, then turned up a week later down on the levee near the river with the stereo tape deck ripped out, and the body all beat to hell. The only part that didn't float was trying to grind me into the pavement. I'd never heard of that happening to anyone. On the other hand, why not a real mean joyrider?

—We got a blood type off the steering wheel. It's not yours, Rat said slyly.

—You checked it, didn't you?

—Bet your sweet pink ass, son. I got a job to do. Maybe you *were* drunk a couple hours ago. Maybe you did go get your lady's car and trash it.

—Who knows what evil lurks in the hearts of men . . .

—Say, Rat smiled,—that's a nice way of putting it. You ever think to be a writer?

—Not that I remember.

Rat patted me on the shoulder.—You'll be all right. Like you say, a little sleep. Call me tomorrow. Maybe we'll have something.

I didn't believe it. He didn't believe it. It was going to go down as auto theft and collision, nobody was going to be found, and the furniture store would have a sale, a brand-new front, and that same damned ugly sofa, cleaned or reupholstered, back in the window again.

The Place d'Armes was one of those small hotels that cater to visitors with rich tastes and thick bankrolls. It was on St. Anne Street, and from the front, you might think it was a renovated private residence for someone who'd made it big in the asphalt or cinderblock business, then hired taste to fix the place up.

The cop dropped me off, and I went inside. The clerk gave me one look and started to reach for the phone. But I had a friend. Tommy C. was bellman there, and over the years we'd done each other some favors. Big shots dropped in, and I got a call. Tommy liked free tickets to concerts and that kind of thing.

Tommy waved the clerk off the phone as he studied me.

—Jesus, you look like you was shot at and missed, shit at and hit all over.

—It's been a long hard day. You reckon we could get past this and I could find a bed?

Tommy shrugged and went over to confer with the clerk. The clerk shook his head. No way. That bastard has to have left a trail of warrants from Seattle to here. Not so, Tommy was telling him. This is a local boy . . . almost a local boy. A great reporter. Undercover. Weird shit. I vouch for him. Fine, the clerk was mouthing. You vouch. At the very fucking least, I want to see money. No checks, no cards. Hard cash. Up front.

—You got bucks, Tommy asked me.

—Uh yeah, I said, trying not to fall asleep in the lobby chair.—How much?

How much was I spent the first hundred and fifty dollars I'd ever put into a hotel room in my life. Plus tip to Tommy. But I thought it might be smart to spend the rest of the night where no one knew I would be. My life's worth a hundred and fifty. To me. Most of the time.

When Tommy took me to the room, I found out why

the high toll. It wasn't a hotel room. It was a small suite furnished with antiques that were something more than old furniture. The bed had a canopy and intricate carving on the headboard, and the wet bar seemed to be made of black slate. Two tall narrow windows overlooked a courtyard filled with tropical plants.

In a few minutes, there was a soft knock at the door, and Tommy trundled in champagne iced down in a silver bucket.

—Everybody gets one, he said.—Unless you want me to swap it in for a quart of Beefeater.

—No, I said,—the way I feel, maybe champagne is the thing.

—That's smart. I tell you about champagne, it makes you feel like a winner.

—Neighbor, I could do with some of that.

—Couldn't we all, he laughed, and handed me a fifty-dollar bill.

—What's this, I asked.

—My piece, he smiled.—I don't stick it to friends. Remember those Sting tickets . . . ?

—I do now . . .

—I got laid three times afterward.

I wanted to ask him how that happened, but I was too dog-assed tired for conversation. I just smiled and waved as he checked out and closed the door behind him. Ah, God, friends . . .

I dialed Denise's unlisted number then. I was glad I didn't have to go through a teenage routine with her father.

—I got bad news and good news, I told her.

—Wes, I can't manage any more bad news tonight.

—The good news is, I'm alive.

—Oh, God . . . the bad news . . . ?

—I almost wasn't. Somebody tried to run me down.

—No . . .

—With your car.

I could tell that she hadn't hung up. There was still that distant hollowness on the line, a low crackling sound.

—I hope you've got collision, I said.—They had to pull your car out of a furniture store window down on Decatur.

—But you're all right?

—I'll always make the sign of the cross when I pass a furniture store.

There was that warm throaty laugh of hers, then. I popped the cork on the champagne and poured myself a glass. I wondered if I could talk her into coming down to join me. I could come up with a few bucks more for that next bottle.

—It's not funny, she said after a moment.—You're funny, but . . .

—Are you getting the idea we've run out of coincidences? I asked her.

—Yes. But God knows what's going on. It doesn't make any sense.

—That means we're not looking at it right. Why don't you come down? We'll drink champagne and figure it out.

—I'd love to. I mean it. But I couldn't get up again— not even if someone were trying to run over *me*.

—Pity. This place looks like an eighteenth-century drawing room. I'll be waking up with the sun in my eyes for a change.

—You're not at home?

—The Place d'Armes. All things considered, I thought I might lay low for the rest of the night. Just to let the coincidences settle.

—I'm glad you're all right, Denise whispered. Her voice told me she was falling asleep.—Will I see you tomorrow?

—Sure. We've still got that feature to finish.

—I was thinking of that on the way home, she said softly.—Could we bring Father John into it? They were very good friends. They lived their whole lives together.

I thought about it for a minute. It was a nice idea. The focus of the story would change, but still, the whole town had known them both, and most of it would be mourning them for a while.

—You want me to come out there? I asked.

Denise hesitated.—No, she said.—I'll come downtown. We'll have breakfast at Brennan's, or do something else touristy. Would you like me to wake you at eight-thirty?

—The next best thing to doing it at six.

—You sound as if you're in a hurry, Wes.

I laughed.—See you in the morning, I said. I heard her hang up, and then another click. That creepy desk clerk was still checking me out. The hell with him. I didn't think anything about it. I was as tired as she was.

I stripped and took a long bath and tried to scrub the blood out of my shirt before I stretched out on the bed. Every muscle in my body was strained, and as hard as I tried, I couldn't seem to focus my mind. I needed to think. The truth was, I needed to write. To put down into some kind of order all the rubbish that was bobbing around like flotsam in my head.

What had Father Cunningham been talking about? "Boys, boys," he'd said. Was he telling me some hoods from the project on the far side of Rampart Street had smashed the statue of Christ and beaten him? Should I have told Rat? Maybe I needed to reconstruct everything the old man said before I went to sleep. Never mind. I'd remember. I didn't cradle a dying priest in my arms every day. "Ash Wednesday . . . if it weren't for your families . . ." Was he telling some neighborhood punks their penance? I had a very heavy penance in mind for them.

But I couldn't hold my eyes open, and I couldn't keep my facts and inferences lined up. I was drifting, sliding toward sleep, and despite the need to think, that was all right. Because even as the room faded away, it came back again. Only this time, Denise was sitting across from me on the bed. She was wearing something shimmering and fragile that revealed almost as much as the string bikini I had first seen her in. The soft light was behind her, highlighting her hair as if it were a halo, so that I could barely see her face. She held up her champagne in an ironic loving toast, her face turned sideways to the light as she tossed her head back and drained the wineglass.

She let me take her in my arms then, the shoulder straps of her gown falling away, the gown itself rippling down to rest on her hips until I drew it off and tossed it across the room. I forgot the dead and the dying and held her close, my lips finding her out, touching her everywhere. She seemed to be wearing the strangest of perfumes, but I paid it no mind, and in a moment our bodies were pulsing together in certain rhythm like the bass drum that sounds endlessly down at the bottom of the world.

CHAPTER
10

THEY SAY THE LONGEST DREAMS LAST ONLY A FRACTION of a second, but there must be exceptions. It was a very long dream, and in it I remember thinking that I never wanted it to end because nothing better was ever going to happen to me in the real world, likely nothing as good. To spend an eternity or two with Denise in that small room was good enough. I almost got my wish.

At first, coming back to the world despite myself, rising up from that darkness in which we had held one another, loved one another for centuries, I couldn't tell if the throbbing rhythm I felt more than heard was that of our bodies close together or that of my heart alone.

Afterward, Denise told me it must have been her, knocking on the door at first, then pounding, finally throwing herself against it, terrified at what she might find when it opened.

When she convinced a passing bellman that she was going to break down the door, wreck the place, and call the police, he used his passkey and let her in. They both almost passed out.

The stench of gas filled the room, and in good movie-style, the bellman broke out a window with a fine old Empire chair. He helped Denise drag me into the hall, and found the open gas jet on the small kitchen range. The bellman said I must be either pretty stupid or very depressed to leave the gas on, and Denise said she told him she was going to break his nose if he didn't shut up. What kind of Uptown communication is that?

I can't remember much of what happened till we reached my place. Then I managed to stagger inside with Denise supporting me. Think of the worst hangover you've ever had. Then multiply it by ten, and add a serious concussion.

I stumbled into the shower with my clothes still on and stood under it for a long time, the cool water playing over my head and shoulders, me taking deep breaths, trying to clear my lungs of the fumes that had seemed like perfume in my dream.

—I would have bet you were the type, Denise smiled as she handed me a glass of V-8, the only thing I could even imagine holding down.

—What? I asked.—Suicidal?

Her eyes clouded over, but then she giggled.—No. I'd have bet you slept without . . .

I must have blushed, because her smile grew wider.

—Shit, I said.

—Don't be embarrassed. I worked as a candy striper at Touro Infirmary one summer.

—Not with me there you didn't.

—It's all right. After all, you saw as much of me the first time you came to the house.

There was something to that. Not much, but something, so I laughed too.

—I must have looked like a side of beef when you and the hotel guy came in.

—I thought you were dead, Denise said matter-of-factly,—and I knew I wasn't going to be able to bear it.

We looked at one another for a long moment. Maybe it still wasn't the right time, but it was getting there.

Then she decided to lighten the mood.

—I gave you mouth-to-mouth resuscitation.

—I'm still a little short of breath.

She leaned over and kissed me, and when she tried to draw back, my lips went with her. When you've been close to death and the essence of what you want your life to be is so near, you turn to it, follow it, reach for it, like a flower does the sun. She seemed a little rattled, as if something had happened that she hadn't expected.

—I was dreaming of you, I told her honestly.—We had a lifetime supply of champagne. That hotel room belonged to us.

—What did we do? she asked in a small voice.

—I don't know what we would have done later, I said.—We never got past making love. It was as if we were both dying of thirst, and we were cool water to one another. I know I was dreaming, but I wanted to stay.

—I wasn't really there, Denise said.

—Oh, yes you were. I recognized your face, your body . . .

She wasn't rejecting it, but it seemed to be moving too fast for her.

—Somebody tried again—I mean, to kill you.

—Yes.

—I should have called Captain Trapp, but somehow I wasn't sure you'd want me to.

—Did anyone ever tell you you've got superb . . . instincts?

—I don't think so. Mostly it's my bottom or my legs.

—Those, too. You were right. I don't want to get hung up with Rat till I have something. He still thinks the business with your car was just some kid joyriding.

—What do you think?

—I think somebody is trying to put me away.

—Then it has to do with Grand-père—and Father John?

—Yes. With whatever your grandfather wanted to tell me. Something Father John might have told both of us. Something worth killing fifteen people for.

—Fourteen.

—Fifteen. If it goes down the way I'm thinking, you can bet Lester Grubbs didn't deal himself that deck of pure heroin on purpose.

Denise looked frightened.—What could be so terrible, so . . .

—If I knew, I'd be talking to Rat Trapp right now. But all I have yet is pieces. Like that call from your grandfather. I still want to know what he could have had to do with the . . . deduction box? He was anti-Long from the start.

—Deduct box. I don't know. It's so long ago. I told you, he only met Huey Long that one time.

—"All that money . . . secrets no one can ever know," I heard myself saying.

—What? Denise asked.

—While you were calling the cops and an ambulance, Father Cunningham went on talking.

—He wasn't conscious, was he?

—No, delirious. But he mentioned money . . . and secrets. What did you tell me Huey kept in the deduct box?

Denise turned pale. We both remembered.

—He said something else. "Bound under the Sacred Heart." What could that mean?

Denise shrugged, but she was looking uncomfortable. As if she knew more than she realized she knew, as if it was bursting to come out. Then she spoke slowly, softly.

—Grandfather's krewe . . . Pandora. They celebrated every Mardi Gras night . . . then, on Ash Wednesday, they put on their Third Order habits and went to a special Mass . . . a Mass of the Sacred Heart.

I shook my head. It felt as if it was all there, now. Only it still didn't make any kind of sense I could understand.

—What's Third Order? I asked.

—The Third Order of St. Francis. You live a secular life, but you take certain religious vows. Members are buried in the Franciscan habit.

I knew there was a connection—not just with Denise's

grandfather lying in his coffin clothed in brown hooded robes, but with something more. It took me a minute or two to dredge up the memory.

—" . . . Murderers every one. Come . . . to do penance. There'll be no end to it . . . Ash Wednesday . . ."

Denise looked frightened.—Wes, what are you saying?

—Nothing. I'm quoting. That's what Cunningham said.

—But what could he have . . .

I didn't answer. Denise was a smart girl. She had to be making the same connections I was. Father Cunningham hadn't been pleading with some ghetto types who'd attacked him. In those last minutes before his battered brain shut down, he was talking about the biggest thing that had happened in his life.

—Have you got a list of the people in Pandora? I asked Denise. It took her a moment to nod.

—I know everyone in the krewe. My God, I've . . . grown up with them.

It was just coming through to her that the people she'd spent her life with might be a criminal conspiracy instead of a carnival club. But for what?

Denise went through a dozen or so names for me. There were others, she said, but she couldn't call them all to mind. They were the sons and grandsons of the founders.

—Eight, maybe a dozen families.

—I guess so.

—Nobody else gets in.

—It's . . . an exclusive club, Wes. You know New Orleans.

—Oh yeah, I answered.—But why that exclusive? Why only those families?

—I never asked my grandfather. He never said. It's always been that way. For twenty-five years before I was born.

—Who's left?

—All the people I told you about. The Lévesques, the Roubions, the Dartoises . . .

—I mean of the founders, the ones who were in at the creation.

—Oh, she said after a moment, her expression grave, sad.—There's only . . . Uncle Henry.

—Henry Holman? I asked.

—Yes. He's my godfather.

She hadn't mentioned him before. I felt my hangover getting worse.

—Holman? publisher of the *Item*? Sure, I saw him in the scrapbooks. How the hell did he get into Pandora? He's not old money.

Denise smiled ironically.—Worse than that. He was one of Huey Long's nearest and dearest. You knew that, didn't you?

I remembered those by-lines in the old files. And a little conversation over the years with other local working press. Just those things you pick up talking in a bar. Henry Holman had been a young reporter back in the thirties. Even though his paper had been anti-Long like the rest of the New Orleans press, somehow or other Huey had gotten the notion that Holman was an honest newsman, that he'd tell things the way they were. As a result, he'd become the only reporter in New Orleans who could see Huey anytime he wanted. He was a kind of one-man news pool. The other newspapermen depended on him to feed them stories they couldn't get any other way.

—It doesn't make any sense, I said.—Why would they take Holman in? He's from north Louisiana. He's not even a Catholic, is he?

Denise shrugged. —He was always at the Ash Wednesday Mass of the Sacred Heart.

Now that she began to think about it, Denise saw the strangeness, too. She could remember that Mass her grandfather took her to year after year—a Mass that seemed to affect him deeply, leaving him shaken, his eyes full of tears not quite shed.

And Henry Holman, seated among New Orleans' finest people, arms folded, face impassive. He did not rise for the Gospel nor did he kneel for the Consecration. But he was always there till the Last Blessing, and

walked out with the others for an austere Lenten meal at
Antoine's, as if it was his duty, and his right too.

I headed for the bedroom to get dressed.—We're going
downtown, I told Denise.

—No, she said tensely,—you're still weak. You have
to rest.

—Not that weak, and I'll rest later.

She came into the bedroom as I finished undressing. I
felt her arms around me.

—I thought we'd stay here the rest of the day . . . and
tonight. What kind of champagne do they serve at the
Place d'Armes?

When she kissed me, I almost forgot the string of
questions I had for Holman. But not quite. I wanted
Denise in a way I'd never wanted anything in my life,
but the old redneck institutions didn't evaporate in the
fire of love. Somebody had made two half-assed tries to
send me on to glory. The next one was likely to be less
subtle, and it could happen while Denise was with me.
Know where your enemies are before you settle down
to sleep, my blood was whispering. I didn't even know
who they were—or why they were. Love was going to
have to wait a little longer.

—I want you, Denise was saying as she touched me,
kissed me.

—If that's what you want, you've got it, I told her.

—Now, she said insistently, as she started to slip out
of her black dress.

I held her hands. If she went any further, I was going
to tell my blood to shut up. You should never do that.
Not ever. The blood can be wrong, but it never lies.

—Later, I said, returning her kiss.

She looked as if I'd slapped her, moving away from
me and walking through the parlor out into the courtyard. I put on a clean shirt and slacks, a blazer and tie,
and joined her.

—I thought there was something, she said sadly.

—More than that, I said.—There's everything.

—Then why . . .

—Because some sonofabitch is trying to kill me, and I

don't even know why. If he brings it off, there won't be anything. For either of us.

We walked into the *Item*, and Vaccaro said Bob Pleasance was looking for me. There was some kind of a Federal Strike Force meeting in Washington about crime on the Gulf Coast that had to be covered. It was urgent.

—Enjoy the capital, I told her.—Don't miss the Statue of Liberty.

By the time we reached Holman's office, I was wondering why I hadn't taken up Denise's offer. Even if Holman was in, he wasn't likely to drop everything to see one of his reporters—someone he didn't even know.

His secretary told me I was wrong. Mr. Holman would see us at once.

The office was standard old-time executive, the kind of thing you still see in big-bucks law firms, not necessarily because the senior partners like the style, but because it's still what clients expect. They'd cut down a small mahogany forest to panel the walls, and the rugs and furniture, the Tiffany lamps with fifty-watt bulbs, the long brocade drapes all chipped in to mention diffidently that they hadn't been shopped for at Sears.

Henry Holman was in his seventies, a big powerful man who looked more like a steelworker who'd made it from blast furnace to main desk swinging his shovel all the way, than a newspaperman. There was something carnal in the way he looked at people. Not just at Denise, who obviously delighted him, but at everyone. As if somehow the whole human population was a potential lunch. He came around the desk and gave Denise a bear hug.

—Honey, it's good you could come by. How's your daddy?

They exchanged some pleasantries. Then he looked at me. It wasn't a hostile look. It didn't seem to take me that seriously. More the casual glance of a man who owns the acreage and spots a gardener daydreaming instead of weeding. I thought to myself, put it away, old man. I'm digging, all right. Then he stunned me.

—Frank Colvin's boy.

—Sir?

—You're John Wesley Colvin. Come down from the *Journal* by way of the *Advocate*. Been here a couple of years. Do good work when something catches your interest. Not easy to interest, though.

Maybe I just stared at him, but I think I nodded. Nobody likes being summed up in a couple of sentences, but he hadn't said anything I could deny.

—Your father was a fine man. Family man. Kind of lawyer who never makes any money. I believe he meant to, but some poor bastard on his way to the penitentiary always came along with a story he just couldn't turn down.

Holman had done it twice in a row. He'd known my father, all right. Not heard about him, had him researched. He must have known him, because he had it all as clear as I did. The only things missing were the feelings.

—He ever tell you he could have worked for me?

—No, sir, I said.

—It's true. I was going to quit the paper and work for the senator in the presidential campaign of 1936. Your daddy said no, he reckoned he'd just keep doing what he was doing. Just as well. Turned out there wasn't any 1936.

The senator was Huey Long, of course. And no, I hadn't known my father had been offered a job with Holman. I hadn't even realized they knew one another.

—Well, that's the old days. Let the dead bury the dead, like the Scriptures say. What can I do for you young people?

I started to tell him the story from line one. He waved me into silence.

—Pick up where you are now, boy. I know about Auguste and John Cunningham. I know about Grubbs. Every now and again, I read my own paper, don't you see.

I told him about the two tries on me, with Denise filling in the details on the second. He nodded and considered.

—Could have been some dumb kid in the little lady's

car. Could have been the damned gas in the hotel room was on when you checked in.

I felt my face turning red, but I said nothing. If we couldn't get something from Holman, we weren't going to get anywhere at all with this thing.

—But, Holman said after a moment,—I don't believe it any more than you do. Auguste had something on his mind. Somebody knows what it was, and he's gonna see you dead before you work it out. That what you've come to?

I nodded, and told him some of what Father Cunningham had said on his way to dying. Holman had been slumped in his chair before. Now he sat up.

—Well, you come on a treasure chest, didn't you? Only thing is, nobody give you the key.

—It keeps going back to the past, I said.—Silly as it sounds, it keeps going back there, to the thirties. . . .

Holman laughed.—Hell, boy, there's no such thing as the past. I mean, except in your mind and mine. They've wrecked most of the cars, and all the cups and saucers are broke up. They've pulled down the buildings and put up new ones. They got all the clothes stored in trunks in the attic. The past isn't even dead. It's disintegrated, dispersed. This is America. Nobody remembers anything past twenty years ago.

—Unless there's money or trouble in it.

—Antique dealers and politicians take care of that. No, what's not gone altogether is scattered all to hell and back.

—Maybe it can be pieced together again.

—You're not looking to report. You sound like you want to be a historian. If somebody's trying to do you something, it's got to be about right now.

Denise and I exchanged a glance as Holman stopped talking. He wore the expression of a man who has finished a task to his own complete satisfaction. This was either the end of it, or I was going to have to come up with a counterpunch. I thought I might have one.

—Where were you when Huey Long was shot? I asked him.—I mean, where exactly?

He stared back across his desk at me for a moment. The satisfaction seemed to have drained from his eyes, and that redneck blood of mine chortled that I had scored one. Not necessarily a big one, but one that had awakened the trenches.

—It's all in the investigation transcript, John Wesley. I was down at the Roosevelt Hotel, sitting out in the hall with Tom Norris, a state trooper who guarded Huey's suite. Huey was supposed to come back that night. He never made it.

—Were you just hanging around—or were you waiting for a story?

Holman grinned.—Both. There was always a story when Huey came to New Orleans. He never let this damned city rest. They hated his guts, and he hated theirs. Two distinct species, he went on.—You've been down here long enough to know that.

—Was the deduct box in the suite? I asked him.

His eyes widened. Solid shot. Smack across the bow. Maybe even a body hit. How could I tell? One beefy redneck face staring across four feet of mahogany at another.

—By God, you *are* a historian. Maybe you ought to be at LSU instead of on my paper.

His hands began playing with some kind of paperweight. One of those old-fashioned things made of glass that contains a scene, a little house and trees, and hundreds of tiny particles. When you turn it over and set it down, snow starts to fall. I could feel his tautness then. Until that last question, his hands had been folded in his lap.

—Was it?

—Nobody knows. If you'd done your research right to the end, you'd know that . . .

— . . . Nobody ever found the deduct box. Right. Was it in the suite?

—Goddamnit, I told you, nobody knows. Sometimes it went with Huey, sometimes it didn't.

I'd gotten things moving again, but I knew I was skating on the edge of being thrown out of the office. I wondered if I'd have gotten this far if Denise hadn't come along with me. It didn't seem like using her. I hadn't made her come. But it still felt uncomfortable. I tried to think as quickly as I could what more I could get out of Holman.

—What was in the box? I asked him, trying to smile.

His smile matched mine. He didn't feel good about the way things were going, but he was feeling better.

—Aha . . . maybe you *are* a reporter. Money and trouble.

—"Money that no one can use, secrets no one can ever know," I said. I heard Denise draw in her breath.

Holman nodded.—I don't know how much there was in the deduct box. But it was early in the month. The rake-offs from state workers would have just been coming in.

—What about the trouble?

—Huey used to tell me he was a man of mercy, of infinite compassion. Said he always turned the other cheek against his enemies. I just laughed, thinking of the dirt he'd done on folks. Still . . .

—Did he say anything definite, name anyone?

—Nope. That wouldn't be like him. He never telegraphed anything. Struck like a cottonmouth. You had a leg full of poison before you knew you'd been hit. I don't know what he had in the box, or who he had it on. It must have been horrendous. Or so they say.

The three of us sat silent for a moment or two, Denise's eyes moving back and forth between Holman and me, Holman in some sort of reverie.

—Never found that deduct box, he said easily.—Long people went to Canada, looked around in Europe. Not a trace.

Then he sat up straight, stared at me, and laughed.

—But I tell you this, son. Big important men went to their graves in Louisiana sweating like hogs in heat, worrying one of Huey's people had that box, and that one day . . .

He eased back in his chair then, portrait of a man who has seen interesting times, lived through them, come to wealth and satisfaction.—That's all past, all history. Hell, what kind of secrets could hold their sting for fifty years?

—There's no statute of limitations on murder, I said.

—Sure there is. There's a statute of limitations on everything. Reckon Jack the Ripper turned up in Surrey? Reckon people would riot to see him hang? Hell, he'd clean up telling it all to the tabloids.

His voice and what he said, that burden of chilled passions, made me believe him. Who the hell would kill for something fifty years gone? It was past imagining. But it seemed to have happened.

—One last question, I said, shooting from the hip. —How is it you got to be a member of the krewe of Pandora?

—Same way anyone gets in a carnival club, Holman shot back quickly. I had the feeling he'd played his hand as long as he wanted to. It was time to get out of the game.—Good friends join together. Or didn't you know?

I laughed at that. Henry Holman had a handle on me, all right. A born-again loner who was playing in the same game with him only because there wasn't another one around.

—I know what's on your mind, he said, almost too quickly.—I was one of Huey's boys then. But this is now. I told you, there isn't any past. Gentlemen come together.

—Yes sir, I said, rising, taking Denise's arm, starting out of the office—wondering to myself just when Henry Holman and the self-styled best and brightest of New Orleans had come together: after Senator Huey Long had been assassinated—or before.

CHAPTER
11

SINCE I WAS DRESSED FOR IT, I TALKED DENISE INTO going to lunch at Antoine's. The food staggers around from so-so to very good, but the drinks are always fine, and I felt like celebrating. I was alive. I was with her. And in a little while we were going to drop by Martin's Wine Cellar, buy a case of a certain champagne, and go home. Just then I still had some thinking to do.

—" . . . If it weren't for your families . . . the awful sin of it . . ."

Denise looked depressed. Maybe she'd changed her mind about the two of us being together always. Always seems to run shorter with wealthy people. They have what they need, what they want, and when something or someone tempts them toward risking it, they pull back into what they have. Even the rich race-car drivers and hang gliders only risk their lives, not their fortunes.

That wasn't something I wanted to think about. What

might or might not be ahead for Denise and me was back burner. I had to figure out what Auguste Lemoyne had wanted to tell me. What Father Cunningham must have known. What Henry Holman seemed sure I'd never dope out. Then, in an instant, my mind whipped around, and I landed on what I'd been trying to get at all day.

—They gave it to him. One of them stole it, and they gave it to the priest.

Denise looked up from her drink, depression gone utterly. She looked frightened.—What are you talking about?

—The deduct box. That's how Holman got himself into Pandora. He was at the Roosevelt Hotel when Huey was shot in the capitol at Baton Rouge. The deduct box was at the hotel. Somehow or other, he helped them steal it. After Long was killed, they stole the deduct box. Then they gave it to Father Cunningham.

—Oh, Wes, you're inventing things.

—Then tell me about Holman. Longs and anti-Longs went to their graves decades later still enemies, didn't they?

—Most of them, I suppose . . . yes. . . .

—Father Cunningham was talking about them, about the people who . . .

My voice trailed away and I dropped a slug of martini down my throat. "Damn you for murderers, every one," the old priest had said. Holy shit, they hadn't just stolen the deduct box.

I leaned over to Denise and caught her arm. She pulled back as if my touch hurt her.

—Tell me about that last day, I said in a low tense voice.—Did anything unusual happen that day? I mean, before Carl Weiss stepped out from behind that pillar and shot Huey Long?

—Not that I remember. There were rumors. People say there'd been meetings. At the DeSoto Hotel here in New Orleans. People planning to kill Long. But that had been going on for years. A lot of silly talk by men who . . .

—Nothing else? Think. No matter how small.

—There's one story. That at one of the meetings, a group of men drew straws to shoot him . . .

—And . . .

—Dr. Weiss drew the . . . short straw.

I gestured for more drinks. I couldn't have eaten then if I'd wanted to. Christ, I was thinking, if all this pays out, it'll be the story of the century. *Item* reporter solves the killing of . . . There I was at the *Times* or the *Post*. All right, Wes. Start with the Lincoln thing. After that, Kennedy. Then my imagination came back south again. In a hurry. Even if it was true, if everything I was thinking was true, how the hell did it tie in with the Bethel Bar? The short answer was, it didn't. I was solving some other mystery. Even realizing that, somehow just then it didn't seem to matter. Maybe there was some connection so deep, so imponderable, that solving the old mystery would open up the new one. There was no other way to go.

Denise nibbled at a pair of soft-shell crabs, and I took on a ballast of martinis. As I drank, I looked around the room. Antoine's had been around since 1847, and this big back room where the local movers and shakers fed must have seen a lot of history. I recognized people at almost every table. Politicians, corporate attorneys, bankers, and developers. The true seed of the men who had determined to see Huey Long into his grave. Or perhaps not quite. I looked from one of them to another, trying to find the face of a man who'd draw straws for his enemy's life. I didn't see any.

But then maybe I wouldn't have seen any if I'd been sitting in that tense hot room in the DeSoto Hotel on a late August day in 1935. Fifty years ago, almost to the day. All I'd have seen were desperate men who thought Long was going to destroy them either by ruining the base of their positions in New Orleans—or by publishing some of those documents, freeing up their closest secrets. Men like those have no special faces. They all look just like you and me.

We drove past the cathedral, but it was closed. A couple of policemen patrolled out in front as if they had been detailed to prevent a crime that had already happened.

—It's silly, Denise was saying as she drove my car past.—Why do you want to go back? I don't think I'll ever want to go into the cathedral again.

—Just this once, I told her.—I wonder if they're having services, I said aloud.—If they are, we could get in with the congregation.

—No, Denise said dully.—They'll have to reconsecrate. They always do that when a terrible thing has happened in a church.

—They must not count crimes of the heart, I said,—or they'd be doing it after every Mass.

—Wes . . . please. I want to go back to your place.

—I want you to show me where they sit during that Mass on Ash Wednesday. I want to know everything about it. What could it mean, "bound under the Sacred Heart"?

—A vow, Denise said.—Some kind of a promise, that's all it meant. Maybe a promise to attend the Mass every year.

—Bullshit. Find a place to park.

We walked back to the cathedral, both of us sweating from the afternoon sun. I wondered absently how it had been inside that room at the DeSoto Hotel fifty years ago. There'd been almost no air-conditioning then. It must have been hot as the insole of hell.

The housekeeper at the rectory greeted Denise with a kiss, hardly paying any attention to me. She couldn't see her way clear to letting us look through Father Cunningham's room, but she walked with us to the cathedral when Denise told her she'd like to say a prayer for the repose of Father John's soul.

There were no police inside, so we knelt in the front pew before the altar of the Sacred Heart. Denise sat stiffly, as if she feared still more pain to come. Then she bowed her head. I had my eyes on the ruined side altar. I didn't feel prayerful, but I was surely meditating. They'd swept up and carted away the wreckage of the statue of Christ. Had the materials from the deduct box been hidden inside it? Was that why it had been smashed? Had they been taken away by whoever had assaulted the old priest? Then I noticed the pedestal where the statue had stood. I thought I could still see the plaster heart lying where I had put it.

My eyes traveled across the sanctuary, over the main altar, to the far side. There were statues located in several places, each on its pedestal. It looked like the pedestals had all been built either at the same time or at least according to the same design. Each was square, made of painted wood, with two levels or steps at the top upon which the statues stood—all but the empty pedestal just in front of me. It didn't have two levels. It had three.

"Under the seal of the Sacred Heart, you hear? All that money that no one can use, secrets no one can ever know . . ." I seemed to hear Father Cunningham's voice there in the hush once more. As if, on the far side of time, he'd changed his mind. It was no longer a door that had to stay closed forever.

I said nothing to Denise but strode past the altar rail over to the pedestal that stood empty now, the rack of candles below all blown out. The two top levels of the pedestal looked just like the ones supporting the other statues. But the bottom one was different. It was larger, more massive. Not enough to attract attention, but obvious. If you happened to be looking for it.

The bottom level looked less smooth, almost as if there were a groove around it filled in less than perfectly with plaster and paint. At the back, there was a small bulge in the finish of that bottom level. What the hell, I thought, all they can do is get me for desecrating a church that's already been desecrated. Pleasance will be understanding. Then I put the scarlet heart of Christ over on the broken altar, took out my Swiss Army knife, and started probing at the plaster and paint.

By the time I'd made enough noise to get Denise's attention, I was done. It was an almost square gray metal box, twenty by eighteen by five, worn and rusted, with an internal lock on one side. My knife wouldn't open it. I was going to have to use a hammer and chisel or a large screwdriver to get into it, but a rush of adrenaline went through me as I realized what I had. And what it made me.

The first man in fifty years to see the fucking deduct box, Huey Long's treasury, his stash—and his dossier on all the wonderful people who had run this splendid town a generation and a half ago. Ho ho ho, I thought. Christmas in August. Pulitzer next year. Wires and nets offering vast new worlds. Then I looked out at Denise.

She was still kneeling in the pew, her eyes fixed on me. No, not me. Of course not me. On the box. The deduct box. Thinking of things that had happened a quarter century before she was even born. Wondering what there might be inside the box that could make all the years she'd spent worshiping her grandfather and Father Cunningham turn to ashes as she read.

—Are you ready to go? I asked her, barely containing my excitement.

She nodded, saying nothing.

—I'm going to have to break this thing open, I told her.—Or get me a locksmith to do it.

We walked very slowly back to the rectory, and Denise told her housekeeper friend good-bye as if she never expected to see her again. Then we went to the car. I stashed the box in my trunk and was about to crank up when a long-haired girl with a face like a bird dog came up and tapped on the window. She worked at Jesus' shop, so I figured she was all right.

—You're Wes Colvin.

—Yeah, I know. What do you hear from Jesus?

—He's . . . somewhere. He needs to see you.

I couldn't make out why she was whispering.

—You got a cold? I asked her.—Summer colds are the very worst kind.

—That's it, she said, looking nervously into the car where Denise was waiting.—A very bad cold. He said you should come by yourself.

—I got to tell you, sis, just now I'm not much for going strange places with people I don't know.

—He said specially if you were with . . . a girl.

—He's out? How did he get out?

—The hard way, she said, her eyes still on the back of Denise's head.—He's not good, Wes. He's hurting real bad.

—Christ, they didn't whip up on him?

—No. Inside. He's been crying a lot. Like somebody broke his heart.

—How far is it?

She didn't even look at me. She kept her eyes on Denise.—A couple of blocks. Over on Dauphine.

I didn't want to leave Denise sitting on the street, but I couldn't pass on Jesus. If the girl was going to lead me into something, I reckoned as long as I was alone and left myself room, I could always run like hell.

—Will you wait a few minutes? I asked Denise.—A friend needs me. Someone who might know more about this mess than we do.

She looked up, and I froze inside.—Don't be long, she said, but her voice sounded as if it were computer-generated, and she looked at me as if she'd never seen me before.

I couldn't do anything about that then. I figured it was just a very wealthy girl coming to realize that she'd almost made a silly mistake—fallen into the wrong bed with the wrong man at the wrong time. I wished I'd let her talk me into staying home. Even without the champagne.

The girl's name was, so help me, Tilly, and we walked fast, me asking her questions to see if she was straight, her answering the best she could, taking two steps for every one of mine just to keep up.

—He just swapped clothes with one of the janitors.

—Come on . . .

—No, he had a hundred-dollar bill in his mouth when he went in. They didn't find it. He gave the guy the hundred, and cracked him over the head.

—What's hurting him?

—I don't know. Look, I work in the shop. I print

T-shirts, I sell T-shirts. Jesus doesn't tell me anything except when to show up and when to go home.

I believed that. Then, before I could come up with any nutcracker questions, we were standing in front of an empty storefront on Dauphine.

—Come on, she said.—He's in back.

—Tell him to come up to the door.

—Look, he's really bad. He doesn't want to come out where anybody can see him.

—Bullshit. Tell him it's gotten real tense while he was inside. I want to see him before I come in.

—Oh shit, man. He's shooting up.

There was that old-time freeze in the blood again. Once, a long time ago, before I'd known him, Jesus had done horse. Not for long, because Ignacio had caught him at it, beaten him half to death, and run him through a very special version of cold turkey. More like cold buzzard, to hear Jesus tell about it. He'd never touched anything stronger than hash since we started kicking shit in the streets together.

—I wish he wasn't doing that, I told Tilly.—But you tell him some sonofabitch is trying to kill me. If I don't see Jesus right out here, with no doors or shadows behind him, I walk.

She went inside. I heard talk. I also looked around for the nearest inhabited door I could dive through if something besides Jesus turned up. There was a pizza joint a door or two down. I thought I could make that. I was getting used to going through doors in a hurry. This one was nicer than the last. It was open.

Then Jesus was looking out at me from large, dark, tortured eyes with even darker rings around them.

—Who? he asked.—Who's trying to kill you?

—I don't know, I said.—Never mind. The girl said you were doing it again.

—The girl should have her tongue pulled out. I been way down. I needed it.

—You look pretty down now. Did they hurt you in there?

—Oh, man, Jesus said.—Oh yes. They did.

—I told you not to do it.

—You were wrong, Wesley. It was good I did it.

—Yeah. The very best. You come out and start pounding skag.

Jesus tried to smile.—Oh shit, skag? My grandpa called it that. Here, you want a . . . reefer?

He offered me a joint. I covered his hand and stepped inside the door.—They're gonna be after you, I said.

—Well, yeah. But it's not a big thing. They're not gonna find me. Till I'm ready.

—You want to tell me what you found out? I've got to go.

—You with that girl? The DA's daughter.

—Yes.

—She's gonna take you down, man.

—Forget it. I'm finding out stuff. I'm getting there. I'm close.

—No, man. You're not close.

—How the fuck do you know?

—I know. Because I'm already there. You do all this silly shit. I went in to where the deal got cut.

He stopped as if he had almost said too much. Then he started to weep. Heroin does wild things with your emotions.

—Christ, he choked.—You know how much I used to love this country . . .

—Was Grubbs in there?

Jesus snuffled for a moment, then pulled himself together.

—Does a whore bare ass? He was in. They had him on dope and parole breaking. He was going back for the rest of that armed robbery hitch.

—Then how? Why?

Jesus shrugged. The girl brought a bottle of gin into the storefront and set it on a table made out of sawhorses and planks. She poured a couple of glasses and we drank. It was as bad as that night at the Bethel, but it was alcohol. Jesus didn't seem to notice. He was looking around the place, tears still coursing down his cheeks.

I could see that somebody had been renovating, taping, and floating the wallboard.

—I was gonna open another place here, Jesus said. His voice was arid, distant. Somehow it reminded me of Auguste Lemoyne's voice when he made that last phone call of his. I wondered if it was the voice of men full of a story they had to tell. Or of men out at the edge, seeing some great death rising like a black sun on the shadowy horizon.

—How did Grubbs get out? I asked.—I need to know.

Jesus shook his head.—No, he told me.—You *want* to know. You don't need to know. Maybe you don't even want to know.

That made me mad. I was sorry about whatever had happened to him in the detox unit. But I was past playing with him. I could see that he was out of it. When I got done, I'd come back and see what I could do for him.

—Look, motherfucker, I said.—Somebody's tried to take me out twice. If you know anything . . .

Jesus nodded. That seemed to make sense to him.

—You ought to ask your girl friend. If you really need to know . . .

—Fuck you, I told him.—If you didn't have anything to tell me, why the hell send for me?

I started out of the place, but Jesus' voice stopped me at the door.

—Wait a minute. Two things . . .

—All right.

—Grubbs wasn't the only one that got out. Look for some spic kid. Long hair. Real good-looking. Took out two men in Austin a month ago. Stone killer. Worked for Santana in Miami. Raúl Gutiérrez. You know what a garrote is?

—No. What else?

—If you can hang in for the rest of today, through the night . . . if they don't get you by tomorrow . . .

—Listen, you dogshit doper, I told him,—I'm gonna be here when they drop your bones down a hole.

Jesus smiled at me. That old beatific smile that said,

No matter what you think, I'm good and I wish you well.

—Yeah, he said.—I know. *Vaya con Dios, viejo amigo.*

I walked out, still bone-pissed. Why wouldn't he tell me how Grubbs got out of Charity? What was the secret? The hell with him, I thought. Down at the end of the road, you're always alone. There are no friends. Only people you know, a few people who may wish you well. From a distance.

I walked back to where I'd left Denise and the car across from the old federal courthouse. In fact, I passed the place once or twice because the car was gone. Maybe she'd had to move on. Maybe she'd make the block and pick me up. Maybe she wouldn't. After a few minutes, I walked down to the Monteleone Hotel and found a cab to take me out to State Street.

CHAPTER
12

IT WAS LATE AFTERNOON WHEN I REACHED THE LEMOYNE house. My car was parked out front. Denise had my keys, so I couldn't check the trunk, but I knew it didn't matter. The deduct box wasn't going to be there.

Carole answered the door looking beautiful and flustered. She tried to tell me Denise wasn't there. I walked past her into the library.

At first I thought Carole had been telling the truth. The library was dark, filled only with soft faltering light from the garden. I walked to the window and looked out. There was still a warmth, a romance about it. I wanted to pretend that Denise and I were out there in the shadows, beginning our life of love. But no one was out there. The lawn was neatly trimmed, the gardenias beautifully modeled by a gardener who had gone home hours ago. I could see where Auguste Lemoyne's marble bench sat, unmoved since he had placed it there in the high noon of his life and his career. But the garden was hot, silent, empty, unpeopled by death and dying.

—Wes, she said from behind me.

I turned and saw her in a corner of the library. She sat in a large leather chair next to a side table. The deduct box was open there beside her. I could see that it had not been jimmied open. It had been unlocked. Denise held up a chain of keys.

—Grand-père's, she said simply.—They were in his room. There's a drawer in the prie-dieu beside his bed.

—He didn't happen to leave a confession in the drawer, did he? I asked.

—He didn't need to. Eight hundred and seventy thousand dollars, Denise said in a small bewildered voice.—In thousands and hundreds.

She spread some of the money out across the table as if she were dealing cards.

—I figured it would be less. Legends never pan out.

—This one did, she said. Her voice broke a little as she lifted one yellowed file folder from a pile of others.

—It's as bad, as ugly, as people whispered it was. And my grandfather . . . made it all happen.

I reached for the folder, but she drew it back, looking up at me, the intense green of her eyes showing even in the gathering dusk.—If you care for me . . .

—How much am I supposed to care?

—Wes, I love you . . . truly I do.

—That's a smart way to feel just now, isn't it?

She ignored it, as if she'd expected me to say something like that.—They're all in here. People I knew when I was a little girl. Everyone in . . . Pandora.

—Your grandfather . . . organized it?

She shuddered, nodded, and I could see that she was crying. I think she had been crying for quite a while.

—Everyone's in there except one, I guessed.—Holman's not in there. He was just a reporter. Huey trusted him.

—Why would Uncle Henry . . .

—Uncle Henry was in on it. That's why he's in Pandora.

Denise looked down, shook her head.—It's like opening a grave, finding out everything's . . . rotten, corrupt.

—That's what you find in graves.

Denise threw her head back, wiped her eyes with a scarf.—You asked me if anything unusual happened that day . . . the day Carl Weiss . . .

—Right. And you said . . .

—I left out one thing. I just . . .

She fell silent. I didn't prod her. It would come.

—That afternoon, Huey phoned the Ingersoll Printing Company in New Orleans. He said he was sending down a lot of documents to be printed, photostated. They were to be done in a hurry, secretly. Only a few of his people knew.

—Goddamn, I said excitedly,—and one of them mentioned it to Holman.

—The printers waited up all night. Nothing ever arrived. Then, in the morning, they found out why, Denise said. She sounded past desperation, almost past caring. I could understand. She'd just lived through the very worst of the mid-thirties in no time at all.

—So Henry Holman was in with the rest of those fine, upper-class New Orleanians, I said.—The rotten sonofabitch knew what they were up to. . . .

She nodded.—They must have offered him a lot of money.

—Maybe they didn't have to. Maybe they just offered him a clown suit and a place on the Pandora membership list. That explains how a reporter gets to be a publisher, I said.

—You don't understand, Denise began.—There was no Pandora krewe in 1935.

—Maybe Henry'll want to fill me in when he finds out I've got the box, I said.—But it doesn't matter. This is going to make one hell of a story.

—He won't print it, Denise said. He can't. He was . . . part of it.

—Right. But the *Shreveport Journal* will. Or maybe the *Morning Advocate*—or the *Times* or the *Post*. I think I just got to be a free-lancer.

—You can't do that, Denise said, rising, moving toward me.—Don't you see? So many people will be hurt, decent people . . .

—Fuck 'em, I said.—These are not my people. I don't owe these degenerate jerk-offs anything. The whole goddamned place is dead or dying.

She spun away from me as if I'd slapped her. Then I realized what I'd said. Even if whatever we'd almost had was over before it began, I was the one who was sounding like a voice from the grave.

—Sorry. The words were wrong.

—It's how you feel, though.

I began picking up the money and folders, dropping them back into the box.

—The attorney general will have to appoint a special prosecutor, I said.—Your father wouldn't want to handle this one.

—There's no evidence there that anyone could use in court. It all happened a lifetime ago.

—Not all of it. Remember the Bethel Bar? And Father Cunningham? Somebody wanted to make sure there wasn't any past, no past at all. Who does that sound like?

—No . . .

I could have read her the membership list of the Pandora krewe, and she'd have said no after every name. Maybe she wasn't dead or dying, but she was part of the walking wounded. I put the box under my arm and started for the door.

—Wes, where are you going?

—I'm going to give Captain Trapp a look at this stuff . . . if Holman hasn't got something else in mind for me before I get there.

—I won't beg you, she began.

—I wouldn't want you to.

—Couldn't you let my father see it first? It would be . . . a kindness.

—So he can tell his friends, and they can start sewing a story together? With you as their chief of research? Is he at his office?

—He's in Baton Rouge. There's a State Democratic Committee meeting. It's very important to him. He'll be back tonight. please . . .

Don't ask me why I nodded. The same reason we offer a toast to dead friends. A stillborn love affair ought to be worth some kind of gesture.

—Okay, I said, one hand on the library door.—Tell him to come by my place. If he decides it's not worth the effort, he can read about it in the paper . . . I'm not sure which one yet.

By the time I'd driven home, my exultation had damped down a little. I was feeling like a shit. Denise had gone through enough in the past few days without my sticking it to her. I was going to walk out of her library with Huey's box under my arm no matter what. But there are ways of doing things. Nice ways, other ways. But when I get excited, the currents of the blood always flow back to redneck country, and my heart and mind just can't help following. We're given to a certain bluntness. It used to be called honesty. Nowadays they call it bad manners.

There was still a piece of the afternoon left when I started in on the word processor with a mason jar full of gin and tonic and a .357 magnum in my lap. The documents spoke for themselves. The story wrote itself.

Sure enough, the old man I'd found dozing the sleep of death in the Bethel Bar had been at the root of it. A stenographer's transcript in the deduct box even re-created conversations in that room at the DeSoto Hotel on the twenty-seventh of August 1935. There were names I'd never heard. But Auguste Lemoyne had been the engine behind the thing. His hand had held the straws six other men had drawn. An obscure Baton Rouge doctor, a family man identified as "Dr. Wise," had pulled the short one.

I sat back in my chair looking out into the courtyard where the summer afternoon was closing down toward evening. I had the place buttoned up tight, and the only way in without ringing was right across my line of vision. Or field of fire. If I had visitors, they weren't going to surprise me. Best for them that they didn't even try to surprise me.

Lord, Lord, I thought. Huey had known everything.

Except the date, the place, neither of which had been specified at the DeSoto Hotel meetings. Perhaps Weiss had chosen them himself. But if a man knows his death has been planned, how does he ignore it?

When the answer came to me, I laughed out loud. I felt a kinship with Huey Pierce Long that I had never imagined.

There'd been threats and plots before, and they'd come to nothing. And at last, he had thought the gutless New Orleans bastards couldn't get their nuts up to do it—wouldn't even make a credible attempt at it. The Kingfish had been wrong, but it was a mistake our kind of men make. And who knows? Except for some secret wedged deep in the soul of that misnamed doctor, perhaps Huey and I would have been right.

For some reason, a host of old north Louisiana sayings flashed across my mind. No cross, no crown. No guts, no glory. Get too strong, you're gonna go wrong. Was some part of me warning myself? It was then that I heard the gate on the far side of the courtyard clatter, and a shadow move across the fading sunlight on the far wall.

When he paused at the French doors, neither of us was really surprised. He didn't seem much perturbed by the pistol pointed at his gut, but then he came from my end of the state. That kind of thing happens up there.

If nobody's ever thrown down on you, you've been living the quiet life. You could have illuminated a banquet hall with Henry Holman's smile.

He stepped inside with his hands out from his sides, coatless, pants held up by suspenders. He turned slowly, with a peculiar grace. The ugliest, dumpiest model for the most shapeless clothes that ever the world had seen.

—That's a nice piece you've done, Wes.

The boys on the city desk hadn't been paranoid after all. The old man did scan the computer files.

—If you like the story, you'll love the documentation, I told him.—Some of the personal motives would gag a maggot.

—Well, that's likely true, Holman said, pulling up a

chair.—Back in 1935, a man could lose it all pretty easy. Little embezzling, mulatto girlfriend down in the Quarter, bastard hid out in Lafayette . . . fond of young boys . . . maybe even your own little boy . . .

He sounded like the deduct box talking. He knew as much as I did. And that damned big smile kept right on coming.

—'Course, that was then.

—And this is now. But it still matters, doesn't it?

Holman shrugged.—I'm the last of 'em, he said.—Old Father John and Auguste and me. Now it's just me.

—You people murdered a U.S. senator, and old man Lemoyne was going to tell me all about it, so you put Grubbs up to . . .

—Whoa. So far, so good. Why don't you just stop there and let me keep a good opinion of you?

—Because you as much as said it. Auguste Lemoyne was going to talk . . . and you're the only one still living who . . .

Holman waved his hand.—Why don't you point out where that gin and stuff is? I know you'd rather I mixed my own.

I waved the pistol at the breakfast bar, and he rose and shambled over to it.—Keep on this side of the bar with your hands out front while you mix, neighbor, I told him,—Or it's gonna run out faster than you can drink it.

—All right, fine, he answered.—Yeah, old Auguste got downright pious when the doctors told him about that biopsy. Said what he'd done had clawed his guts for years. Cancer was just the . . . what'd he call it? Oh yeah, the temporal punishment for it. He went to Father John, told him how he felt. Damned priest said, Well, if that's how Auguste felt, if that's what he had to do . . . John never had a lick of common sense.

—Auguste confessed to Father Cunningham . . . ?

Holman laughed as he came back to his seat with his own mason jar.—Shit, and I thought you were a smart boy. What the fuck was there left to confess to Father John? Auguste had done that on the tenth day of September, nineteen hundred and thirty-five. And Father John damned near blew the whistle on all of us right then. That very day.

—But he didn't. . . .

—Nope. Too many innocents, Father John said. Had him a very fine conscience. Counted up as how it would ruin the wives and children.

Holman paused and drank. Then he leaned back, put his feet on the edge of my desk. I didn't complain. He wasn't much of a threat in that position.

—There was times I'd just about as soon he *had* told.

—You're going to tell me about *your* conscience.

—In a pig's ass I am. I slept okay then. I still do. But Cunningham drove a hard bargain . . . or hadn't you figured out just what the krewe of Pandora was . . . is?

—You mean it's . . .

—The good Father called it a penitential society. We could cover it up any way we wanted, but every damned one of us better show up at the altar of the Sacred Heart every Ash Wednesday.

—Or . . . what?

—Guess. One year we had to carry René Lévesque in there like a bag of groceries. Poor sonofabitch died two days later. And the young ones, the boys, joined as they got older. Most of 'em didn't know what it was all about, but Father John said we had to bring 'em along. Called it a chapter of the Third Order of St. Francis.

His expression changed then. I couldn't tell if it was old frustration or lingering amazement at the price New Orleans' best people had had to pay for fifty years.

—You realize? We didn't know where that damned priest had put the box after Auguste went simpleminded on us and handed it over to him. If somebody had had enough, the deduct box would turn up at the U.S. attorney's office the next day. He had his ways. You can't go fucking with the Church.

I couldn't help laughing.—So you went to Mass every Ash Wednesday . . .

—And begged forgiveness—or acted like it—and prayed for the repose of Huey's soul. Ain't that the stone-ground shits? Prayed for Huey's soul. . . .

—You knew what Huey had in the box, and you sold him to them like a sack of potatoes.

—Yeah.

—Why?

Henry Holman found that smile of his again. He raised his hands, palms up.—Why not? he asked me.

—Christ, I said. It appeared I still had the capacity to be astonished.

—Like that TV show, the price was right. Look, they were going to do what they were going to do. Hell, by the time Auguste came to me in the hotel that evening . . .

—What evening?

Holman looked at me as if I were an idiot.—I believe we're talking about Sunday, September eighth, nineteen hundred and thirty-five. Around nine-thirty in the evening.

—You didn't know anything till then?

—I gave the New Orleans boys a little news from time to time. Not a lot. Just enough to keep my hand in on that side of the board. Somebody mentioned Huey was about to clean out his enemies. I had told Auguste that.

—That's all you knew?

—Hell, I knew what every other dumb bastard in the state knew. They were talking killing down in New Orleans. No, that's not so. I knew one thing more from Auguste. Some of them had drawed up their guts. They really meant to do it. If Weiss hadn't got him, they had 'em a second and a third plan. When the clouds build up, it's gonna rain.

—And you were shopping for an umbrella.

—That's a good way to put it. Shit, when Auguste showed up at the Roosevelt, he said it was happening *right then*. Not maybe, not even gonna. *Happening. Then.*

—What did you do?

—I got Trooper Norris to go have him a beer downstairs. Said I'd keep my eyes open. I did. I stood outside the suite and kept lookout. Afterward, I didn't say anything. Auguste did the rest. Got the box, wherever it was.

I shook my head.—Christ, I said.—You knew . . .

Holman shrugged.—The way I saw it, New Orleans was where I was gonna make it—if I made it. See, I never had the *Times* or the *Post* in mind. Too far from home, and they don't pay all that good.

Holman contemplated my gin, and drained the jar.

—I'm gonna have one more quick one, then I got to drop by home before I go to the paper. My wife likes to see me. Hard to believe a woman would give a damn fifty-one years in, ain't it?

—You got Grubbs out of Charity detox, and pointed him at the Bethel Bar like a missile, I said. Then I realized my finger was tightening on the trigger. I eased back. Henry was going to have to try something before I could close the books on him myself. He turned from the bar shaking his head.

—Well, like I said, maybe you're a historian. But you're a piss-poor reporter.

—Good enough to put your ass in the chair for mass murder, you old sonofabitch.

—Why in the hell would I do that? There's nothing in the deduct box to tie me in to . . . what they did to Huey. If all this past-and-gone bullshit ever comes out, I'll deny everything I just told you. They'll have you in a straitjacket before they put me in a cell.

—But people will realize . . .

—Piss on what they realize. I'll deny, deny, deny. I'm seventy-nine years old. I got more money than I got arthritis pains, and that's a lot. I don't give a good goddamn what anybody thinks anymore. You got any other motives in mind?

I frowned. Because I was believing him. But there was no alternative. He had to be the bridge between that infernal room in the DeSoto Hotel half a century ago and the Bethel Bar.

—I didn't come to throw myself on your mercy, son, Henry said as he touched his drink with Rose's Lime Juice.—You ain't got a thing I need, and you still got the Bethel Bar business to figure out. But there's other people with tender feelings. About the past.

—Tough shit, I said.—One of those folks put aside his

feelings and wiped out a barroom full of people. It still could be you. The hell with all of 'em. Let God sort 'em out.

Holman shrugged, eased up out of his seat slowly.

—Well, it's getting to suppertime, and I still got a full night down at the paper. By the way, I coded your story as quick as it came in. Nobody's gonna see it but me. And you. People don't want their daddies and grand-daddies remembered as killers. You can see that. When you decide to kill the story, it'll be easier that nobody knows but you and me. No use alarming the troops, is there?

What had he said? *When* I decided to kill the story?

—I'll never kill it, you miserable bastard. Not ever.

He studied me with the kind of indulgence you save for a bright kid who hasn't quite pulled it all together yet.

—Never say never, he chuckled.—There ain't no such thing as never. There's less to never than there is to . . . history.

He walked out into the late afternoon, across the courtyard. I stood at the door watching him go, studying that shambling bulk of his. I doubted I'd ever see his like again.

—You gonna give me the code word? I called out to him.

He turned and smiled back at me. The same smile he'd been wearing coming in.

—Wesley, I think better of you than that. You already *know* what the code word is.

Then he was gone, and I went back inside, sat down, and stared at my portable computer screen. While we were talking, it had gone blank.

CHAPTER
13

HOLMAN LEFT ME JUST THE WAY HE WANTED TO. uncertain of everything. No, that's wrong. Not quite everything. I knew for certain what Auguste Lemoyne had wanted me to know. Holman might swear he'd never said it, but that didn't matter. I knew the truth of it. That mattered.

But if Holman hadn't been behind the killings, and the two tries on me, who had? I hadn't written Holman off. He was as sly as his blood kin in north Louisiana and Texas who had created fortunes in oil, manufacturing, finance through a combination of hustle, confidence, and sheer nerve. Maybe he'd walked into my courtyard reckoning on whizzing one right past me. Hell, he'd suckered Huey Long. Why not me?

But it didn't sit right. I believed him when he said he didn't give a damn if everybody in Louisiana knew he'd played Huey false. He'd rather it didn't happen—him and those other anonymous folks with tender feelings.

But would he set out to kill everyone around him for silence?

Then I tried it another way. Start from the two tries to put me out of business. Holman hadn't known where I was or what I was doing. Unless he had that other Latin—Gutiérrez—sitting outside the paper waiting to track me to Denise's car. That's when I stopped pacing and fixed myself a drink.

Because I realized there was another scenario. Denise had given me the keys, asked me to bring her car to the house. And Drew Lemoyne had overheard.

Either of them? Both of them? I tried to go back and see it another way, but the blood drummed and told me to go on, I was doing all right.

What about the hotel? I hadn't even decided to go to the Place d'Armes till I left Rat's office. Had the same creep followed me again? That was one way. But I'd called Denise. She knew where I was. Had she asked the name of the place? I couldn't remember. Then something clicked. Literally. I remembered that small sound after she'd hung up. Like there'd been an open extension while we talked. But how did the room clerk tie in?

I think I gave up about then. I understand deduction is a noble art. Maybe I'm just no good at it. I kept coming up with serial possibilities, and no way I tried could I rule Denise out of the series.

The hell with it, I thought. I threw down my drink and switched off the computer. Maybe Rat was right. I should leave detecting to detectives. I picked up the phone and called. It was time to fill him in. At least he wouldn't charge for professional advice.

Rat met me, and we went to a bar nobody associated with the Uptown crowd could have found with beaters, bearers, and elephants. The Kit-Kat Klub. I told him a tale that widened his eyes. Then I passed the deduct box over to him. When he saw the money, he nodded like an elder of some archaic tribe.

—I tell you this, son. All the time you were talking, I thought you were jiving me. I swear to God . . .

—Eight hundred and seventy thousand reasons to believe, I told him.

Just then, one of the resident bloods walked by. He wore a washed silk suit, a hat with a large feather in it, and a pair of those damned one-way sunglasses.

—What you looking at, motherfucker? Rat snarled at him.

—What you got there, brother?

—I'm not your brother. And what I got is your nuts. Any time I want 'em. You hear?

—Easy, my man, easy. I'm going away.

—Bet your black ass you're going away.

Rat calmed down and sifted through the files in the box.—It's so goddamned . . . weird.

—Why do you say that?

—'Cause all this fits. Before that field hand come by, I was gonna tell you . . .

—Tell me what?

—One of my people found that ass from the detox staff at Charity. The one who took off for California.

—Alphonse. So . . . ?

—He got himself a nice piece of money for dumping the records on Grubbs.

—Holman?

Rat shook his head.—Naw. A guy named D'Anton. Chief of staff at Charity. Told Alphonse it was all a mistake. Wanted the records dumped so Grubbs couldn't sue the hospital for unlawful restraint. Let go another dip name of Gutiérrez at the same time. Wasn't no big thing to Alphonse. Said they did it all the time. For one reason or another. Alphonse is steadily improving himself.

It was my turn to be surprised. I remembered Hugh D'Anton angrily talking to Drew Lemoyne in the emergency room after Father Cunningham had died.

—Something else . . .

—What?

—That MAC-10 . . .

—The submachine gun . . . ? What about it?

—We always do a secondary ballistics run. Sometimes you find out the same gun was used in another incident.

—Okay.

—That piece was logged in to the police property room a year or so ago. Killing down in the Ninth Ward.

—Somebody stole it from the property room?

—If you mean broke in and made off, forget it.

—Walked in and walked out? Some cop?

—Cops not the only ones go in there, honey lamb. Forensics, ballistics, coroner's office . . . and, oh yeah . . . people in the DA's office.

—You know D'Anton's a member of Pandora? I asked him.

Rat stared at me.—No. Same outfit as Holman?

— . . . and the Lemoynes. Father and son.

—Well, what do you say. Father and . . . son. Ah . . .

—What? Don't leave me hanging.

—Police records on Grubbs got scrambled.

—That's what Jesus said. I figured you'd find out.

Rat gave me a mean look.—Shit, little buddy. You checking on me?

—No, I just . . .

—Never mind. Somebody got to the computer.

—Who?

—Well, there's staff and operations, forensics, ballistics, the coroner's office . . . and . . .

—Shit. The DA's people . . .

—Uh-huh . . .

—Denise said her father was in Baton Rouge. Some big Democratic meeting. She expects him back tonight.

Rat laughed.—Big meeting . . . Yeah, sure. They're all huddled together up there to pick their candidate for governor.

—You mean . . .

—That's what they say, Rat nodded.—They say Andrew Jean-Baptiste Lemoyne is gonna run. And if he runs . . .

—He wins.

—Looks like. You wouldn't bet the farm on the other side.

—No. Unless . . .

—Christ, Rat breathed. We stared at one another, speechless.

—Naw, Rat said.—That's bullshit.

—I didn't say a goddamned thing. You thought it all by yourself.

—You don't know what I was thinking.

—A man couldn't get elected in Louisiana if it came out . . .

— . . . his old daddy had planned the killing of Huey Long. You could run Mussolini against him . . .

— . . . and win. Walking away.

We drank for a while, letting it sink in. Neither one of us believed it. Which is to say it ran against our prejudices. After a while, Rat spoke, one word following another with great care.

—Would a man kill his father to keep it from coming out?

—What if his father was already dying? What if he only had weeks, months, to live?

—But all those other folks, Rat mused.

—You pick Lester Grubbs to do your work, it's a fuckup from the start, I told him.—You tell Lester, waste him in an alley, out on the street. But Lester has a grudge against Sandy . . .

—Maybe. Or maybe our man figured one murder among a dozen would just go on by.

—Reckon we ought to drop by Lemoyne's place? Maybe he's home by now.

Rat was thinking.—Not just yet. You got to set these things up. When I go see the DA, I got to be walking in with a pat hand.

We drove out to what they call old Metairie. Just inside the Orleans parish line. It's not as old as Uptown, the Garden District, or University. But you don't live on food stamps out there. The homes are large, the lots spacious. Old Metairie says, *Je suis arrivé*. With a slight American accent.

Dr. Hugh D'Anton lived on Garden Lane. It was a dream street with ancient oaks dripping with Spanish moss, Italian cypress, magnolias three stories tall, and wide manicured lawns. What it lacked in tradition, it made up in luxury. It took bucks to get there. It took more to stay. Dr. D'Anton had made it quite a while back. I reckoned he had in mind to hang around. *Je suis y je reste?*

The black man in the dark suit wasn't the first butler I'd ever seen, but they don't make up a large class even among the New Orleans rich. This one Rat happened to know.

—Eisley, he said, as we stepped inside,—I know you and you know me.

—Yes, sir.

—I want you to go tell the doctor that Mr. Drew Lemoyne is here. Say Mr. Lemoyne is all shook up. Say he's got to see the doctor right away. You understand?

Eisley didn't understand, but he nodded and moved off into the guts of the house somewhere.

—You think he'll . . .

—He'll do what I told him to do. I had him on bunco six years ago. Before I moved to homicide. Sonofabitch give back the money, and I give him a ticket to ride.

—But, then . . .

—Shit, Wes, there's always new evidence. When you get hold of a man in this business, you got a little piece of him for good.

Rat knew his business. In a few minutes, D'Anton came into the foyer almost running, talking rapidly as he came.

—Goddamnit, Drew, you know better than this. What are you coming here for? I've done all I . . .

Then he saw us. I thought he was going to faint.

—Christ, he said, supporting himself against the banister of the stairs.—Oh, Christ . . .

—Well, yes, Dr. D'Anton, Rat said smoothly.—I can see where you'd say that. I'm Ralph Trapp, NOPD. Would you rather talk here or down at Central Lockup?

D'Anton decided he preferred his solarium. I walked among the plants, stared out the polished windows into a semitropical rain forest of palms and vines, Spanish

bayonet, banana and rubber trees, purple and white
wisteria, elephant ears, and candle trees.

—We got hold of Alphonse Delattre out in Torrance.
He said to give you his best, Rat was saying. I had my
back to them, so I could afford to smile.

—He explained how you told him to dump the records
on Lester Grubbs and Raúl Gutiérrez.

—Well, yes, but you see . . .

—Doctor, excuse me. Right now I believe I got your
ass on thirteen, fourteen—maybe even fifteen counts of
capital murder if I can show you passed that pure heroin
to Grubbs.

—Christ, D'Anton said again. When I turned, he was
sprawled in a tasteful striped canvas lawn chair. His
eyes looked like cracked saucers. His mouth hung open.
Rat paused, seemed to be considering. After a moment
he shook his head.

—You know what? Maybe you ought to get hold of your
lawyer. The more I think about it, the more I think . . .

—Listen, D'Anton began in a tremulous voice.—Listen, I didn't do anything. I mean, the records . . .

Rat nodded sympathetically, then drew a small plastic
card from his vest pocket.

—''You have the right to remain silent. If you choose
to talk, anything you say may and will be used against
you . . .''

—No, please . . . So help me God . . .

—Who, Doctor?

—Who?

—You didn't wake up one morning and say, I better
scrub those records. Hospital might get sued.

—No . . .

—Who?

—If I tell you . . .

—I don't do no deals, Doctor. But if you help me
make my man, I believe you'll be home free. Fucking up
public records is the very least thing he's done.

D'Anton looked as if Rat had thrown him the last
available rope from a lifeboat bobbing in the ocean. Two
hundred feet from the *Titanic*.

—The . . . district attorney said there'd been a mistake, and . . .

—Bullshit. That version gets you indicted.

—He said Grubbs and the other one weren't . . .

—". . . if you cannot afford an attorney, one will be appointed . . ."

—He said his father was going to . . .

—Tell what your folks did to Huey Long fifty years ago.

D'Anton looked astonished and relieved all at once.

—Yes, he said, his voice breaking.—How did you . . .

—Never mind. We know the whole mess.

—All . . . of it?

—Did he tell you what he had in mind for those two boys to do?

—No. He . . . said I wouldn't want to know. So help me God, if I'd had any idea what was going to . . .

Rat stood up, nodding.—I believe that. They say you're a good doctor.

—I try. . . .

I decided to take a shot of my own.

—The night Father Cunningham died, I began. Rat looked at me with surprise and amusement. I smiled right back. I'd gotten my confidence back. Anyhow, I wasn't going to get another chance to impersonate a homicide detective.

—Yes, Dr. D'Anton answered. He wasn't in a mood to ask for credentials.

—I saw you talking to Lemoyne. You seemed angry, upset.

D'Anton nodded.—Father John . . . baptized me. He baptized my daughter . . .

—What did Lemoyne say?

—He said . . . we were in too deep to . . . to be sentimental. That it was . . . almost over.

Rat and I exchanged a look. D'Anton covered his face with his hands.

—Shit, Rat said coldly.—It hasn't even begun.

*   *   *

This time, Carole looked frightened when she answered the door. As if she thought Rat and I might be dangerous.

—Miss Lemoyne isn't here, Mr. Colvin. I mean, this time she's really not here. She's gone up to Baton Rouge.

—Right, I said, and pushed past her into the house.

Rat moved in behind me, and elbowed Carole into a corner.—I got some questions for you, miss, he started in, his voice as smooth and chocolate as her skin.

While he talked to her, I went through the whole place from the kitchen to the bedrooms. I think I knew she wasn't there. I wanted to see the way she lived, the places she passed through every day. When I reached her bedroom, I stopped. It wasn't what I expected. The room was just above the library so it overlooked the garden too, only from a higher elevation. The furniture was understated, expensive, without decoration. There was a bookshelf filled with history books, legal textbooks, and pamphlets. On the table beside her bed was a photograph of Denise and Auguste Lemoyne on the night of the Pandora ball in 1978. Barring the difference in their ages, the two of them looked more like sweethearts than grandfather and granddaughter.

Except for the picture, Denise was nowhere to be found. It was as if she'd never been there at all. It made me wonder why she had gone to Baton Rouge—which of my scenarios was true. And the more I wondered the more I realized I had to find out.

Back downstairs, Rat was wrapping it up with Carole.

—You've been helpful, Miss Laborde, he was saying with a light touch on her hand.—If you should hear from Mr. Lemoyne or his daughter . . .

—Of course, Captain.

—I wouldn't bet on it, I told Rat as Carole turned back toward the rear of the house.

—Your girl got restless. Went through her father's desk till she found whatever it was she was looking for. Then she lit out.

—Passports? I asked.

Rat shrugged.—You reckon she knew all along? She's in on it?

The way he said it pulled me up short. I didn't want to believe that. Uptown ladies are all actors. Their whole damned lives are badly written plays of one kind or another. But Denise loved her grandfather. If I knew anything about her, I knew that. Didn't I?

—You want to drive on up to Baton Rouge? Or would it be a waste of time?

—I believe I do, Rat said easily.—Lemme make a couple of calls. I need me a warrant and a man in East Baton Rouge parish.

It was almost an hour before we got on the road. Rat had to drive by the home of a district judge. It seems his honor had difficulty with the idea of issuing a warrant for the Orleans parish district attorney.

When we finally squared away, the moon was up, and the trip on the interstate was a lot quicker than going by way of Airline Highway—the old route, the road Huey had built, the way his people had come up to Baton Rouge from New Orleans that night when they heard he had been shot.

—History, Rat mused as we drove over swamps and flatland.—I never paid no attention to it. I always had in mind where I was, what I was doing.

—That's history, too, I told him.—Right now is history making itself.

Rat leaned back behind the wheel and considered that.

—The night fifty years on, when they drove north to close out the Long murder case. Oh, man . . .

—Not murder. Assassination. Murder is what happened at the Bethel Bar. Assassination is . . . different.

—Yeah. I guess.

—Assassination is when they try to kill history, to keep it from moving past them, over them. Or when they try to end it.

—Anybody ever bring it off? Rat asked.

I looked out at the moonlit land passing by. It had suffered us all since the beginning. Indians, Frenchmen, Spaniards, Englishmen. Fishermen, hunters, trappers, farmers whose nationality was a mystery even to them.

Dream after dream, hope after hope, flag after flag. Doom after doom.

—I don't think so, I said.—Not that I know of.

We could see the capitol building in Baton Rouge long before we reached the city. It glowed in the distance, standing out beyond the twisted architecture and burning gas flares along Scenic Highway that marked refineries and chemical plants owned by the interests Huey Long had fought against when he first became governor. Then we moved into traffic, gliding off the interstate and down onto Government Street. I knew the way from my days on the *Morning Advocate* a long time ago.

As we came closer, the building Huey had built to house his administration, his legislature, his plans, rose out of the dark city like an Art Deco cathedral. It was bathed in floodlights, and as we parked in front, I turned and looked across the way to a dark mass of granite and bronze. A metallic Huey Long stood gesturing from a tall firm pedestal.

Jake Slater, the Baton Rouge detective, was waiting on the capitol steps for us. He was businesslike. What the hell did he care who we had come for? It wasn't his business. His business was jurisdictional. He told Rat he had an East Baton Rouge judge standing by if it was necessary. I think he assumed I was another Orleans parish cop, the way D'Anton had.

—You arrest your own DA's often? Jake asked Rat.

—Not as a rule, Rat answered smoothly.—Most of 'em have pretty good control.

—Yeah. Putting a lawyer away must be a pain in the ass.

—Not as bad as a cottonmouth. Worse than a horsefly.

—Haw . . .

There was a state trooper at the door. He ushered us inside, saying that Mr. Lemoyne was in the governor's office. There had been a long Democratic party conference. It had lasted most of the day and on into the night.

—Making plans for us, the trooper smiled.—Deciding who's gonna get the governor's chair next.

Rat grunted.—What do you bet they're gonna have to

do it all over again? We got another place for Lemoyne to sit.

The trooper gave him a questioning look, and took us down the dark hallway.

—Did a young lady come in earlier? I asked.—Lemoyne's daughter?

—Yeah, the trooper said.—She didn't get in. They sent out word she'd have to wait.

He gestured at a bench halfway down the hall. Someone was sitting there, but only a few lights were on, and I couldn't see who it was. As we drew closer, I could make out Denise. I stopped by the bench. Rat and the others passed on toward the outer door of the governor's office.

Denise looked up and saw me. I think she tried to smile.

—Did you come up . . . for me? she asked.

I wanted to say yes, but I think she knew better before she asked.—No, I told her.—We're here to . . . see your father.

She didn't look surprised. She simply nodded, holding her purse close to her body. I noticed that she was dressed in black. Or maybe she had been since her grandfather's death, and I simply hadn't noticed.

—Holman came by my place. We talked for a while.

—Yes, Denise said, her voice distant, thin, serene—as if somehow the pain and loss had begun to subside.

—Look, I don't want you hurt anymore.

—Thank you, Wes. That means a lot. I'll always remember that you . . . didn't want me hurt.

I was looking for words to explain what we had come for, some way of letting her know what was about to happen to her father before Rat arrested and cuffed him.

If she was involved, I didn't want her to make some silly move. If she simply let things happen as they had to happen, no one would ever know. Except me. But even as I fumbled, realizing that there were no words to ease this last anguish she would have to undergo, I heard a door open down the hall.

—Something else, Denise was saying.

—What?

—I wanted you to know. . . . I left a note with Carole.

—She didn't give it to me.

—She wasn't supposed to. Until . . .

—Denise, what are you talking about?

—My father . . . tried to have you killed.

—He told you that?

—He didn't have to. I thought about everything that's happened, and . . .

Denise was looking past me then, even as she talked. Her eyes were suddenly bright, penetrating, as she heard what I heard. I half-turned and saw the outer door of the governor's office open. There was laughter from inside, and the voices of men whose speech was full of confidence and certainty. Then someone stepped into the hall.

—Oh, Wes, she said as I was looking away,—I wish it could have been different for us. Will you remember that?

The rest passed so quickly that I was still dazed, uncertain later when I tried to remember what had happened.

I felt a movement at my side and turned back to Denise. She was standing now, her eyes burning down the dark corridor toward that single, slim handsome figure who had emerged from the governor's office. She held her purse in one hand, the other inside. As I tried once more to tell her what even then was happening—no, about to happen, on the verge of happening—I saw her purse fall away to the floor, and in her right hand was a small pistol.

She said something I couldn't hear as she brushed past me, walking rapidly down the hall toward the man who stood alone, still talking to someone inside the governor's outer office.

It took me a moment to register what I had seen, to start after her, to stop her from whatever she had in mind, no matter what it might cost me. I remember all that passed through my mind was, *Don't let her be hurt again. Not again.*

It was a variation on that dream again. A passageway as long as the journey to Proxima Centauri, stretching down past the governor's open door to a vanishing point of dim light, Denise breaking into a run there ahead of me—in the direction of her father, who was still talking to someone within the office as a block of shadow that had to be Rat Trapp, Jake Slater, and the state trooper detached itself from the opposite wall and began moving toward him from behind. And me, feet mired in some viscous fluid called time, the substrate—or effluent—of history, struggling, thrashing, trying to catch up with Denise.

But then, by some grace I still don't understand, I broke free from time and history just long enough to catch her arm from behind, to send her sprawling on the cool floor, and to pull her, still struggling, into my arms.

—Let me go, she cried out.—I know everything, and I can't stand it.

Yes, you can, I said or thought as I held on for all I was worth and a little more, looking down the corridor to where Lemoyne and the others stood out in a frozen tableau illuminated by light from inside the governor's door. They turned and looked down the corridor our way. They began moving out of the light into the shadow toward us. I twisted the gun from Denise's hand and shoved it deep into my pocket as I held her fast with my other arm.

I was lifting her to her feet, trying to think of some explanation for having tackled her—as if such a thing was worth noticing just then—when I saw, halfway between Lemoyne and the others and Denise and me, a blur as someone in a white suit moved from behind a pillar on my right, and stood before Lemoyne as if to question or accuse him.

Then came the first shot, and I saw nothing more. If I had identified the report by sound alone, I would have had to say it was a shotgun. It seemed to grow in volume, to intensify until it rolled across and through Denise and me, collapsing into echoes as it sped toward vanishing points before and behind, at the ends of the corridor, the culminations of the world.

When the second one came, and the ones after that, I was on the floor, covering Denise, hearing the pop and snarl of ricochets as they passed by overhead or sounded off the marble walls on either side. After forever, there was silence for a moment. No, not silence. Because there was still the sound of Denise's sobs coming from beneath me.

Then yells, feet running, and a moment later the corridor was flooded with light. Someone had hit the main switch. The capitol was open for business again.

I lifted Denise to her feet, held her close for a moment. Then we walked slowly down toward the knot of men who stood talking, crying out, gesticulating, around two bodies lying on the marble floor.

Lemoyne was bleeding from the mouth, his eyes rolled back. Someone, maybe Jake Slater, was tearing away his tie, trying to pull his collar loose, finally ripping the button away in his haste.

Rat squatted beside the other body, the one in the white Palm Beach suit. I let go Denise and stepped closer.

Rat pushed his hat back and looked up at me as he slipped a .38 police positive back in his shoulder holster.

—Oh, man, I'm so goddamned sorry, he said.—I never been sorrier in my life.

I knelt down beside Jesus and lifted his head into my arms. I wanted to talk to him, but he was past that. There were four or five wounds in his chest, and one bullet had smashed his jaw. Even so, the family resemblance was astonishing. His eyes were still open, the pupils enormous, and even the wreckage of his face below took nothing from the ferocity, the primordial triumph still shining up out of them.

—*Vaya con Dios, viejo . . . ,* I started to say. But even as I did, the fire in his eyes dwindled, began to die. In another second, Jesus was gone, and I was holding a corpse in my arms.

As I let his body down to the floor and reached out to

close his eyes, to do for him what I had not done for his brother, above or below the excited talk and chatter around me, I heard one voice out from the others. It was choked and stammering, as if the one who spoke was coarse, mannerless, talking through a mouth full of food.

—Why . . . why did he shoot me? Lemoyne was asking someone.

I turned and saw that Jake Slater was supporting him, holding his head up. Lemoyne was staring across at me, at Jesus. The front of his expensive shirt was soaked with the blood still pumping out from beneath it.

—Don't you know, you stinking sonofabitch? I yelled across the distance, realizing even as my voice went out of me that I was talking to a dead man.

CHAPTER
14

H OLY CHRIST, SOMEONE SAID IN DISMAY,—SOMEBODY
shut that bastard up.

Rat helped me to my feet, and shoved aside some fool
who had resented my words and wanted to make something of it. The man fell backward on the floor. No one
paid any attention to him.

—This ain't our town, this ain't our scrap, Rat whispered to me quietly, firmly.

I tried to pull loose from his grasp. Not a chance.

—Now, I don't want to have to hurt you, he said.
—But this hasn't got nothing to do with you. You'll see
that later on. You coming on out with me nice, or would
you like a groove across the back of your scalp?

He began muscling me down the corridor. But we
both saw Denise at the same time. She stood staring
down at her father's body from a few yards away. Slater
had covered Drew Lemoyne with his jacket, and Denise's feelings seemed just as veiled by her expression.

Rat gave me a hard nudge in the ribs.

—How about we see the lady home? No need anybody know she was even here, is there?

—No, I said.—I guess not.

—Now you're getting yourself together, he said smoothly.—I'm gonna go talk to Slater and that trooper. You get her out to the car. Do it now, 'cause in about five more minutes the fucking place is gonna be zipped up tight. They'll be taking statements till next year sometime.

Rat walked back toward the commotion. I took Denise's arm and led her outside. We both paused on the steps. The air had turned cool, and there was lightning on the far side of the Mississippi. There were things I wanted to say to her, but it was no good. It was too late. Or maybe there never had been a time for us. When she spoke, I must have winced.

—I knew you'd come, Denise said woodenly.

—I didn't know you would.

—You don't think well of us. You never have.

—I think well of you, I told her.—The hell with the rest of them. They'd have covered for him. He'd have had the best lawyers money could buy.

—He won't need them now.

—He won't need anything, I said.

—That's not quite true, Denise said, looking up at me, her eyes distant and dead. Before I could ask her what she meant, Rat was standing beside us.

—Okay, she wasn't here. But that only holds if we get her home with no newspeople finding nothing out. Lemme take her in the police car. You can drive hers.

I wanted to alter the arrangement, take Denise with me, but Rat shook his head. I understood what he had in mind. No one in the parishes between Baton Rouge and New Orleans was likely to stop a police car. I took Denise's keys and went looking for a badly mangled Mercedes 280 convertible.

The way I made it was by pretending it was just a late-night drive in a fine car. I put the top down and let the breeze whip across my face as we headed back south again. A little distance out of New Orleans, it began to rain. I pulled over to put the top back up, and Rat moved out ahead of me. By the time we hit Orleans Parish, I'd lost them, and the rain had started coming down hard.

When I got to State Street, it was still falling, filling the gutters, standing in the street, beginning to inch up over the sidewalks. It was one of those late-summer torrents that washes the place clean for a few hours. After it passes, you can smell the air the way it must have been on a morning long ago when the Sieur de Bienville stopped along the river and decided, miasmal swamps, humidity, mosquitoes and all, this was the place.

Rat had pulled his car into the drive and under the large sheltered area at the side of the house. Through my windshield, I could see Denise get out, hesitate, then start inside. Rat followed her. He was carrying something bulky under his arm. I noticed there were lights on inside, to the far right of the house, where the library was.

I sat in the Mercedes for a few minutes. Except that it was raining and I needed a ride from Rat, I told myself I wouldn't go in at all. Tonight had finished it. Denise had lost everything. Whoever, whatever she was going to be, would be starting with tonight. She owed no one anything. Least of all me.

By then the rain had slackened, and I walked up to the house and inside. The side foyer, which I'd never seen before, was empty, but I followed voices across the house. As I reached the main foyer, someone with a black bag was walking up the stairs. It was Hugh D'Anton. He looked down on me, I up at him. No sign of recognition passed between us.

They were in the library, of course, but it wasn't quite who I expected. Rat and Henry Holman sat beside the long library table with a carafe of brandy and three glasses.

—Bad news travels fast, I said, for lack of anything better. Holman looked up from the deduct box he held open in his lap, shook his head with a humorless smile.

—You call fifty years fast?

I didn't say anything. He had the box. I looked over at Rat. His expression was benign, detached. I kept staring at him, but he wasn't going to get uncomfortable. He'd been made uncomfortable by experts with assault rifles. He was out of my class.

—Here, Holman said, pouring a glass of brandy. —You need a good slug of this. It's been a bad couple of days.

I reached over and took the brandy because I needed it. My hand was shaking, and I wished I could cut it off.

—I get this feeling . . .

—Yeah, Henry said pleasantly.

— . . . that it's not over yet.

—See, he smiled at Rat and tapped his head.—This boy works for me. He's got him a hundred megabytes in there, and it's tooling all the time.

Then he turned back to me, the smile fallen away.—We want it to be over, Wes. Tomorrow's *Item* is gonna tell folks how their DA was killed by a dope fiend with a grudge. Drew's dead, and there's no reason to dig any deeper. Let tonight be the end of it. Kind of give it the status of . . . history.

—Which is to say, nothing at all.

Henry Holman's eyebrows knitted, but that old grand-dad smile never faltered.—I got to say my opinion on that has changed some the last few days. But never mind.

He lifted an attaché case from beside his chair and set it on the table. It looked new, with gold fittings and soft, dull-polished leather. A nameplate just above the combination lock had initials: JWC. Henry opened the case and pushed it down the table toward me. It was filled with packets of hundred-dollar bills.

—If you and I was gentlemen, we could just look at that and smile at one another. Then you'd get up and take hold of the satchel there and walk away.

—But we're not, I said.—We're not gentlemen. Not you, not me.

—That's true. So you go on and count while I tell you about it.

I lifted one of the top packets, then the one below that. It seemed there were eight or ten layers of bills. I think I wanted to cut off my hand again.

—One million, Holman said easily.—Which is more than eight hundred and seventy thousand. That's yours. And this, he said, tapping the deduct box,—this belongs to certain local folks who kicked in all that money. Call it a deduct from Pandora's box. Now you can get up take your satchel, and start walking.

—Local folks like Hugh D'Anton . . .

—Local folks who haven't got names. Who never reckoned that fool Drew Lemoyne would go so far.

—No, I croaked.

Henry looked mildly surprised. I heard Rat whistle through his teeth. Holman looked over at him, a new expression of feigned bewilderment on his face.

—Well, Captain Trapp, you got any suggestions?

Rat's smile was broad and fine, tinged with a certain comtemplative distance.

—Now you got to understand, Mr. Holman. I can't really have an opinion because I'm not here. Been gone half an hour or more. You could find me at the Kit-Kat Klub.

—Funny you'd say that, Holman answered.—I been home asleep for hours.

I came up out of my seat.—There's got to be something in the air around here, I heard myself saying. —Some chemical in New Orleans. It turns men into shit.

It never even reached them. Holman just nodded and indicated the attaché case with his eyes.—Don't hold your breath, son. Just take what's yours and go wherever you want to go.

—Whatever's right, I said, and reached for the deduct box. Holman's hand caught my wrist. I never felt a stronger grip in my life.

—I don't want the fucking case, I yelled.—I want what I found. I want the truth.

I pulled the deduct box loose from Holman's grip and

started for the closed door of the library. If they were going to stop me, they'd have to do it the hard way.

—Captain Trapp, I heard Holman say in a tight voice,—I believe Mr. Colvin's making off with material evidence in the murder of Father John Cunningham.

I turned back at that. I thought I was about to receive my postgraduate degree in cynicism. Rat was looking across at Holman with that same mild, bemused expression he'd worn ever since I came in.

—Before you make your mind up, Captain, I expect you ought to know what's on the line. A lot of the better people think you're ready for superintendent of police. And one day before long, maybe mayor. I believe we could back a man who knows what it means . . . to protect and serve.

Rat nodded. Then he looked up at me, and back to Holman.

—You sure can read folks, Mr. Holman, he drawled.

—I like to think so.

—I'm a man with a plan.

Henry took a deep breath and pulled himself from the chair.—Well, a man like that has got to make political decisions every day. You just made your first one, Ralph, and I'm proud of you.

Holman walked toward me, his hand outstretched for the deduct box.—Come on, son. Don't make it a police matter.

Then Rat's voice stopped him in his tracks.

—Except I haven't made any decision, and that box won't make it as evidence. We don't need it.

Holman turned on him.—What the hell are you talking about? Colvin took it from the cathedral. It's the motive for John Cunningham's killing.

Rat shook his head.—We got prints in the cathedral. Some junkie named Gutiérrez with a rap sheet from here to El Paso. Found a couple of candlesticks from the altar in his room. One of 'em had blood on it. All we got to do now is find him. We will.

—Gutiérrez? You know damned well Drew Lemoyne sent . . .

—Ummm. Mr. Lemoyne got him sprung from Charity all right, but what are we gonna make of that? Parole boards, judges, DA's—they all make mistakes. Anyhow, Rat went on slyly,—you don't want to get into Mr. Lemoyne's motives. Do you?

—Goddamnit, whose side are you on?

—Mine, Rat said, his voice as smooth and even as before.—My side. See, when I make that political move I've got in mind, I don't mean to owe any sonofabitch on earth—least of all your kind of sonofabitch.

Holman looked suddenly much older. He seemed to sag from the inside. Rat looked at me and motioned toward the door with his eyes.

—I believe you were gonna go do whatever it is you mean to do, he said.

—Right, I answered, tucking the box under my arm, starting out of the room again. As I closed the door behind me, I heard Rat's voice once more.

—And whatever it is you mean to do, make sure you do it right.

I was almost out the door when I remembered one last thing. I took Denise's pistol from my pocket and set it on an old marble-topped table in the foyer. Someone would discover it there and put it wherever it belonged. If I'd managed nothing else right for her, I'd kept her from doing to her father what her father had done to his. That had to be worth something. Didn't it?

When I reached my place, the rain started in again. For half an hour or so, I looked through the documents in the deduct box. Except for the file on Auguste Lemoyne and his co-conspirators, the dark secrets so many people had feared for so long seemed tame. Or was it simply the way I saw it, perspective of an age in which anything less than mass murder seemed hardly more than bad manners, and even mass murder forgettable after a decent interval.

The sound of rain falling, overflowing the gutters up above, called me back from that past. A wet breeze blew in from the courtyard, and I looked out there where light from my lamp fell on the flagstones. They seemed to dance and shiver under a film of water as each new wave of rain shook the trees and sifted soft light over the uneven, sculpted rock below. *This is not history,* I remember thinking as I watched. *This is real.* As if somehow the immense past that had come to claim us, looming out behind us all, as permanent and solid as the flagstones under a film of ephemeral water, was truly no more than a fiction agreed upon.

I was on my second mason jar of gin and tonic, sprawled in my chair, almost released from thought, when I remembered that I was still, despite everything, a reporter. I should have gone back to the *Item.* Eyewitness to the assassination of an important public official. By morning, Holman would have sent word down through the sewers of command to Pleasance and I'd be fired. But not yet. Not just yet. Rat had said whatever I meant to do, do right.

That had to mean finishing what I had started. Write Drew Lemoyne's story as I had written Auguste's. Murderous son of a murderous father, son who murdered his father. Himself murdered in the name of a murdered brother by one then murdered by the law. I already had the lead: *It is said of many men that they would do anything to rise to power. But it is true of very few.*

The story wasn't going to see print in the *Item,* but the state was full of other papers, and with something like the evidence in hand, maybe I could push it directly to the wires. Something like the evidence?

Even as I cranked up my portable computer and dialed in the mainframe at the paper, I wondered if I could retrace Drew Lemoyne's steps. Even if Rat would be willing to twist Dr. D'Anton's arm and prove Grubbs and the other one had been released, their records dumped, on Lemoyne's say-so, that left the rest of the evidence to pull together. I'd need corroboration. I had to be able to show by another independent source that Drew had known his father was about to reveal what Auguste and the other members of Pandora had done so long ago, had known of it and was determined to stop it—no matter what the cost. That could only come from one place: inside the Lemoyne house, inside the Pandora circle.

Denise? Forget it. At the end of it, she'd be as determined to protect Auguste Lemoyne's name and reputation as she had been to blow her father into hell for killing him.

Servants? Had Carole heard a quarrel between them, threats? And if she had, why would she tell me?

What about the housekeeper at the rectory? Was it possible she had overheard something said between Auguste and Father Cunningham? Still again, the same question: why tell me?

I took a long pull on my jar and shook my head. It wasn't going to happen. Whoever I might try to reach the next day would already have been reached. Either tonight—or half a century ago. There'd be a wall as blank as the one raised in the wake of Huey's death. I felt a thrill of anger coursing through me. The sonsofbitches were going to bring it off again. Drew Lemoyne might be dead, but he was safe. He was going into the family tomb as a fighting DA cut down by the brother of a big-time dealer.

As I was thinking, I typed the name I had given the file into the computer. For a moment, the screen remained blank. Then it stuttered and sent me a message:

FILE CODED——USE CODE NAME

I hit the keyboard with my fist. Holman had told me he'd code-locked the story. Sure he had. Why leave it wide open for anyone who happened to look into my computer drawer for something? He'd probably even locked out Pleasance. Then I remembered. Holman had said I'd know the code. But I didn't, and I was too damned tired to begin typing in words and combinations of words randomly.

It was over for me in New Orleans. I had a box full of documents that would likely be authenticated at the end of months of research by independent scholars—for whatever that was worth. I had lost a friend, a job—and the best story anyone was likely to get in the measure of a single lifetime. I had almost lost a girl, too. But you can't lose what you never had.

On the other hand, I also had eight hundred and seventy thousand dollars. I might have some trouble explaining it to the IRS, but Holman and his friends weren't going to scream. Every bill in the box would be dated 1935 or before. From Holman's perspective, the sooner I spent it all, the better. Because the bills helped to authenticate the files. Nobody ever attempted to push forged documents by salting them with almost a million bucks in old bank notes.

That kind of money made a hell of a consolation prize. I could go where I wanted to go, do what I wanted to do. I was free of this damned rotten town and its people that Huey had loathed so much.

Then why wasn't I phoning for airline tickets? Why wasn't I packing? Why did I feel like a loser instead of like the newest member of the little rich?

Because, I thought, the money doesn't mean anything. You always assumed you could make as much money as you needed, as much as you had any business with. You can use some of the money to send Jesus home, and some to buy a card for Denise that says, Get Well and Good-bye. Then what?

I was thinking about mixing myself another jar, getting blind drunk and working it all through the next day, when it hit me. I came out of my chair as if someone had nudged me with a cattle prod. It wasn't over. I wasn't finished.

The whole damned thing could still be proved. That spic Gutiérrez who'd been released from Charity along with Grubbs, the one who'd tried to take me out twice, was still on the street somewhere. If Rat stayed on it, and they picked him up in Denver or Orlando or Jamaica, he'd talk. He'd be looking for the best deal he could make to avoid being tried for the priest's murder. He'd say that Drew Lemoyne had turned him loose and sent him after me. That would do it. Because the answer to the question of why Lemoyne wanted me dead lay in the deduct box. All the slender, time-worn evidence, the assumptions and inferences, all of it would fall into place if Gutiérrez talked.

I was pacing up and down the room like a lawyer in front of the toughest jury he'd ever faced. I thought through it all one way, then another. It kept coming out the same: it wasn't over. Gutiérrez could sew it all together. If Rat could find him.

For a moment, I thought to call Rat, tell him what was riding on Gutiérrez. Then I decided there was no reason. It was almost dawn, and nothing was going to get done in what was left of the night. I set down my jar and took off my shirt. All of a sudden, I was as tired as I had ever been, as I ever expect to be. I smiled. It didn't matter. A man without a job is like a millionaire. He can sleep as late as he wants. Anyhow, I thought, I fit both categories.

I switched off the computer and the lamp at my desk. In the soft light I stood listening to the rain still falling outside. But I saw that garden once more, Denise stepping from the courtyard into my sight, kneeling beside a gardenia bush, her body slender, tanned, full of life. I saw her hands reach out for a bloom. Then I tensed as the doorbell buzzed. And that's the last concrete thing I can claim to recall.

What happened next is more of a dream than a memory. I dreamed I was moving toward the door when I felt a terrible slashing pain in my throat and lost my breath. I tried to yell, to turn, but all that came out was a gurgling sound as if someone was choking to death. I think I must have kicked over the table where the jar of gin was setting as I reached back and managed to get hold of someone's wrists. As I was falling I remembered something Jesus had asked.

—You know what a garotte is?

I remembered then, and it came to me that no one would have told Gutiérrez that Drew Lemoyne was dead. Or if they had, then the contract must have been renewed.

I landed on the floor on my back, hearing noise far away, cries, pounding on a distant door, as I looked up and saw above me an angelic-looking Latin with long dark hair who was expressionlessly strangling me to death as my hands weakened and lost the struggle to tear away the wire around my throat. Then, as the dream and the mind that bore it began to fade, I saw one thing more. Above him, behind his shoulder, Denise's face, her eyes burning downward at me as they had toward her father in that shadowed corridor of the capitol where he died.

CHAPTER
15

I MUST HAVE LOST CONSCIOUSNESS THEN, BECAUSE THERE was a sharp break between that last moment and the next in which I was breathing again, a band of pain around my throat as if someone had severed my head, then reconsidered and put it back where it belonged. When I opened my eyes, the room was dark, and something heavy lay on top of me.

It took me a minute to pull myself from under Gutiérrez's body. When I was able to sit up, I stared down at the same face that had been poised above me a few moments before. His eyes were open, and there was something like a smile on his lips. As I remembered what had been happening, I tensed and jerked my legs out from under him. He rolled over, and I could see the two spreading dark wounds in his back. After I got to my knees, rubbing my neck and throat, my mind began working again. It sure as hell wasn't me who had shot him. My .357 was under some file folders on the work-table beside the computer keyboard.

In my life, I'd never been so thirsty. I climbed to my feet and stumbled over to the breakfast bar to get some ice water. Then I remembered thinking I'd seen Denise's face behind Gutiérrez. I drank slowly, painfully, trying to figure out what had happened. There's a certain curiosity that won't go away when you've come back from the edge of . . . history?

There's no way to tell how long I stood there sipping the ice water as fast as my throat could handle it, and musing as to why I was still alive. The dizziness and fatigue hadn't left me, and as I leaned against the bar, I wondered crazily if I could just leave Gutiérrez where he lay, go to bed, and sort it out with Rat Trapp in the morning.

I didn't need a doctor. The sonofabitch hadn't cut my throat or windpipe with his wire. Aside from the pain, my main symptom was a pair of hands that shook so badly I couldn't make them do what I wanted. After I'd gotten down a quart or so of water, holding the glass in both hands to keep from dropping it, I wanted a drink. Warm gin would be fine.

Even in the dark, I knew my place well enough to fumble my way over to the pantry, where I kept a gallon of gin. I had stepped around Gutiérrez's body and was almost there when I heard someone breathing raggedly nearby—or maybe I'd been hearing it all the time and my mind had just cleared enough to register it.

I tensed, then dived back across the room, landing square on Gutiérrez, clawing at the edge of my work-table where the .357 magnum lay. I came up with it clean and cocked, took a couple of rolls and stopped, lying on my belly near the center of the room, aiming out toward the doors that opened onto the courtyard, facing the larger part of the room, where the sound seemed to have come from. I swallowed hard and felt that pain in my throat, bright and sharp, again. If Gutiérrez had brought friends, I was going to fill the god-damned apartment with corpses. I had lost too much in the last few days. I wasn't going to lose anything else. Least of all myself.

—All right, motherfucker, I croaked as loud as I could.

—Step right up . . .

It was as if my words had stopped time itself. The sound of breathing wasn't there anymore. Even the dripping of water from the eaves seemed to have vanished. I was too mad to be afraid. All I wanted was something to shoot at.

—Wes . . . help me . . .

Later, I'd have time to wonder why I hadn't hesitated, told her to show herself, done the things I knew to do if I wanted to make sure of losing nothing more. Just then, I didn't think anything at all except that she might be hurt. I dropped the gun and found what was left of my lamp. When I turned it on, I still couldn't see her.

—Denise . . .

—Wes . . .

She was sitting on the wet flagstones outside in the courtyard. Her robe, tied over a flimsy silk gown, was soaked by the rain. When I reached her, the pistol fell from her hands into a pool of standing water. Her eyes seemed enormous, full of horror and pain much worse than what I'd been through. Some of the water coursing down her cheeks was rain, some wasn't.

—Are you hurt? I asked her.

—Oh, God, I hurt so much, she whispered.—And it's never going to end. Not ever . . .

—Yes it is, I told her.—It already has.

I picked her up and carried her in to my bed. Her hair was soaked and twisted, and if she had been wearing makeup the rain had washed it away. She shivered uncontrollably.

—Please hold me . . . just hold me.

I did what she asked until she fell asleep. Then I covered her with a blanket, got up, and poured myself a drink. As quietly as I could, I tried to put the place back in some kind of order, righting the table, propping the broken lamp against the computer.

It was turning light in the east when I picked up

Gutiérrez's body and dragged it into the courtyard. I found an old drop cloth I'd used once to paint inside and covered him with it. The misty rain soaked through, turning the cloth dark so that I couldn't tell whether it was discolored by water flowing down or blood welling up. It occurred to me again that he had been the end of it, his the last testimony that could tie it all together, make it credible, force that long bitter story into the light. Auguste Lemoyne's killer was dead, and now so was Father Cunningham's.

In a day or so, they would be burying the man whose ambition had awakened the past like dormant plague in an ancient tomb. It was an incredible story. I sat down and finished my drink, trying to think of where I would like to go to start things over again. After the story was written, after the truth was down in black and white—whether anybody would publish it or not.

The day dawned fine and cool, and Denise woke up with a start as the sun touched my bed. I brought coffee to her, kissed her hair, and held her for a moment.

—Dr. D'Anton gave me a sedative, she began, then found her hands shaking so that she could hardly hold her cup.—But I had to come to tell you . . . And when I got here, that man was . . .

—I know, I said.—What was it you wanted to tell me?

—I'm leaving New Orleans. I'm going to Europe for a while. . . .

—I understand.

—No, you don't, she said, beginning to sob again, looking away from me.—You don't understand. I'm leaving because . . . I don't want to be in the way.

—In the way?

—When you write your story. When somebody publishes it. I can't stand to be here, to hear what people say, but . . .

—Why do you think anyone would publish it? I asked her.

She looked up at me in surprise.—Why? Because . . . it's the truth.

—Yes, I said,—it's the truth.

—I hate it that people will remember him that way.
—Your father . . .

Denise laughed, her eyes full of that fire I'd seen twice before.—I don't give a damn what they think of him. He was . . .

Then that breeding of hers cut in. She shrugged, shook her head.—Auguste Lemoyne was a good man, she said coolly, as if she was beginning a lecture in Louisiana history.—He truly was. You never knew him. He was . . . very precious to a little girl who had no mother . . . and no father, either.

She rose from the bed then, with a flash of perfect legs. She stretched toward the sun, and then turned back to me. Her hair was curly and tangled from the night's rain, but I had never seen her lovelier, more desirable.

—I came to tell you that . . . I mean, if there's still anything between us, the story won't ruin it. Afterward . . . if you came to Europe . . .

Her voice trailed off. Denise wasn't used to leading when she danced. She looked like an anxious little girl as she waited for me to answer. I stood up and took her hands in mine.—You just changed all my plans, I told her. We held each other and kissed.

I took her home then, and called Rat from her place. Denise wanted to dress and go back with me, but I told her it wasn't going to be that way.

—Go ahead and dress, I said.—I'll be back when I get everything done.

Back at my place, the forensic people were finishing up. One of them who had seen me twice before in the last day or so gave me that curious look again. Rat was dressed in a seersucker suit accented with a regimental tie. He was sitting in the courtyard with a glass of lemonade beside him, a fine Panama hat in his lap.

—I believe you need a special unit of your own, he said drily.—Or maybe when we can't find some nasty bastard, we ought to put you out on a string like catfish bait.

I told him how it had gone down, and he nodded.

—She did a good thing, he said.—A man couldn't ask for a better woman. Gimme the gun. We already got that piece of wire he liked to use.

—You don't have any problems with it?

—Oh, yeah, he laughed.—I got the problem of romancing the medical examiner into certifying the motherfucker got shot in front. With a .357 magnum. Other than that? I got no problems at all. What the fuck, man. You think you're the only Southern gentleman in these parts?

—I'm not thinking at all right now.

Rat looked like a thought had just struck at him.—I damned near forgot . . .

—What?

—I owe you an apology. You were right all along.

—Right? About what?

—Gutiérrez. He's . . . he *was* a Colombian. How do you do it, Mr. Colvin?

Maybe we laughed longer because we both knew it was over. Done with. All but the history of it.

—By the way, thanks for last night, I said.

—That bullshit with Henry Holman? What'd you expect? Whoever's nigger I am, I sure as hell ain't his. I don't need that sonofabitch. Pretty soon he's gonna need me.

Rat got up to leave then. At the gate of the courtyard, he turned back and gave me a long, serious, calculating look.

—'Course I'm still interested in seeing how you do what it is you got to do.

—What? I called after him.—What's that?

But he was gone, and that was all right because I knew what he meant.

I went inside and puttered around, cleaning up the last of the mess, trying to think of how to do best what I knew I was going to do.

I had to explain it to myself. That was the hardest part. Because I knew I would always be an alien in New Orleans, with no love for it, no understanding of its ways, nothing but the deepest contempt for what it counts as good. I thought of the hills and piney woods around Shreveport and the Texas border, of that certain killing edge that made rednecks what they are, that had made us love Huey Long, warts and all. I could hear the coursing blood booming within, and the sound of it said truth, truth, truth.

At the heart of me, I had always reckoned one day to find my own Alamo, to go down as Jesus had in the midst of blazing guns doing some great good that men would recognize, that would stand somehow even when the memory of it dimmed into legend, and the names and the place were forgotten.

Then I thought of her. Not simply of a girl who had appeared for a moment in her nearly naked beauty in a garden to pick a blossom and place it on a marble bench. I thought of her as she was now. I remembered what she had said to me in the shadowed corridor of the capitol as she made ready to do her own great good. Before Jesus had come to take the doing out of her hands.

—Oh, Wes, I wish it could have been different for us. . . .

She has no one now, I thought. No people, no home. No one. And who the hell do you have? Can you tell me the name of your home? Or the great good your revelation is going to serve?

I sat down at the computer, booted it, typed in my own ID and then

PANDORA

I wasn't surprised when the story came up. I'd have been downright amazed if it hadn't. I hit a couple of keys, and the computer responded with something like surprise:

DELETE TEXT?——ARE YOU SURE?

—Yeah, I said aloud.—I'm sure.

Then I hit the execute key and watched history dissolve before my eyes.

It was an hour or two later when I parked Denise's car outside the house on State Street and went up to the door. Carole gave me a special smile as if, despite everything past, I was her favorite visitor.

—Miss Lemoyne is out by the pool, she said.—Do you know how to get out there?

—No, I said.—It's my first time.

Carole nodded sweetly.—Come along, she said.—I'll show you the way.

We walked through the kitchen and out a passageway into the garden. I looked back over my shoulder at the windows of the library as I passed the gardenias. I reached down to touch the marble bench in the shade of an ancient magnolia.

Then we stepped through a narrow passage in the tall hedgerow, into the sunlit courtyard where Denise sat under an umbrella at a glass table beside a long sparkling pool. Carole turned back, and Denise rose to meet me. She still looked pale, but I hardly noticed. She had on that white string bikini she'd been wearing the first time I'd seen her.

—I didn't dress, she said with something like a smile.—Is it all right?

I took her in my arms, kissed her shoulders.—It's better than all right. Here . . .

I handed her an envelope. She looked at it curiously, then turned back to me.—That's the Tulane University crest, isn't it?

—I would have gone to LSU, I said.—But it would have kept me away from you too long.

—I don't understand, Wes. What . . .

—Maybe you should open the envelope, I said.

Denise took out the single sheet of paper, read it curiously, then looked up at me, tears welling in her eyes.

—Oh, Wes, darling . . . how could you?

—I think you've got it backwards.

—All the documents are sealed in the Tulane Library . . . until 2035?

—That's the agreement, I said. I handed her the other

envelope. She seemed almost dazed as she drew out the two signature cards and read them aloud.—The account of Mr. and Mrs. John Wesley Colvin . . . eight hundred and . . .

She pulled me down to her and kissed me hungrily, as if for the first time in a very long time she had nothing to fear at all.

—It's all over, she whispered.—It's really over, isn't it?

—That depends on what you mean, I said.—The past is going to have to wait for fifty years. The future begins right now.

About the Authors

John William Corrington is a distinguished Southern novelist, poet, and scholar. He has written more than ten books, including the novel SHAD SENTELL. His wife, Joyce H. Corrington, is a former chemistry department chairwoman of Xavier University. The authors have collaborated on numerous film and television scripts. They live in New Orleans.

Attention Mystery and Suspense Fans

Do you want to complete your collection of mystery and suspense stories by some of your favorite authors? John D. MacDonald, Helen MacInnes, Dick Francis, Amanda Cross, Ruth Rendell, Alistar MacLean, Erle Stanley Gardner, Cornell Woolrich, among many others, are included in Ballantine/Fawcett's new Mystery Brochure.

For your FREE Mystery Brochure, fill in the coupon below and mail it to: